WINNERS
AND
LOSERS

SPELLBINDERS
FEARON'S FINEST FICTION

WINNERS AND LOSERS

Dan J. Marlowe
David St. Vincent
William Warren
Steve Bradley

FEARON EDUCATION
500 Harbor Boulevard
Belmont, California

Simon & Schuster Supplementary Education Group

SPELLBINDERS™
FEARON'S FINEST FICTION

Chamber of Horrors
Changing Times
Cloak and Dagger
Combat Zone
Foul Play
Strange Encounters
Under Western Skies
Winners and Losers

Cover Illustrator: James Gleeson

Copyright ©1991 by Fearon Education,
500 Harbor Boulevard, Belmont, CA 94002.

ISBN 0-8224-2806-7
Library of Congress Catalog Card Number: 90-82216
Printed in the United States of America
1. 9 8 7 6 5 4 3 2 1

Contents

The Hitter

Dan J. Marlowe

1

Eddie Rivard came down for breakfast and found a note from his father on the table. "Open up the cage early," it said. "A scout wants to see young Bluth hit against the machines."

Eddie nodded to himself as he filled his cereal bowl. Young Bluth was Tom Bluth. He had been a freshman at the local high school when Eddie was a senior. In the past three years Tom had become the best young fielding shortstop in the entire county. But in the batter's box, he had yet to show much talent.

Eddie finished breakfast, picked up his keys from the hall table, and went out the screen door. He walked 200 feet to the nearby field and unlocked the batting cage.

Years ago Eddie's father had had a great idea. He had set up a batting cage and a golf driving range back-to-back on their property. It had made them a comfortable living ever since.

Eddie walked over to the pitching machines. Then, as he did every morning, he serviced each machine with oil and a fine layer of grease. When he was through he walked back to the batting cages. He switched on the power in the last cage.

Way out behind the pitching machines was a canvas backdrop. It stopped everything hit out there. The balls dropped down into a slanted gutter at the base of the canvas. The gutter rolled the balls toward a sunken box alongside each pitching machine.

Eddie picked up a bat and settled himself into the batter's box in his left-handed stance. Then he pushed a button to have a ball pitched. He watched it go past him. He always watched the first ball to judge its speed and spin. Even the machines gave the ball a certain amount of spin.

Then he touched the automatic button to keep the balls coming. They arrived every 10 seconds. Eddie swung easily. His first swing drove a line drive over what would have been second base on a real baseball field.

The machine pitched and Eddie hit. Most of his swings resulted in solidly hit balls that reached the canvas in a hurry. Eddie hit for 20 minutes, stopping twice to reload the machine. When he heard the outside door open, he turned off the power.

As he turned around, he saw his father and Tom Bluth walking toward him. With them was a beefy-looking man Eddie had never seen before. The man's face was bronzed from years in the sun. He had a belly that hung over his belt, but he looked like an athlete. Or an ex-athlete.

"Joe Daly, this is my son Eddie," John Rivard said when the three approached. They shook hands and Eddie nodded a greeting to Tom.

Sweat beaded Tom's forehead, although it really wasn't hot yet that early in the morning. "He looks nervous," Eddie thought.

"Joe scouts for the Cubs," Eddie's father said.

"Don't be trying to give me a big head," Daly replied, laughing. "I scout for the Cubs' Double-A and Triple-A teams, and you know it."

"Whatever," John Rivard shrugged. "Grab a bat and step in there, Tom."

When Daly's back was turned, Eddie moved the speed control back a notch. The first pitch wasn't exactly a floater, but it didn't hurry up to the plate, either. Tom swung and fouled it off, straight back.

Daly spoke up immediately. "Is that all the horsepower that thing's got?" he complained. His voice was gruff. He seemed like a no-nonsense type of man.

Eddie had tried to help Tom look good, but his trick hadn't worked. He winked at Tom and moved the control back to where it had been. They certainly weren't going to fool Daly about the speed of the pitched balls.

The pitches came up to the plate and Tom swung hard at them. Too hard, Eddie thought. There was the occasional crack of a well-hit ball. More often there were pop-ups and sliced foul balls mixed in with a lot of misses. Tom was lunging at too many pitches. It kept him from making good contact.

Eddie kept a poker face and tried not to let on that Tom was doing poorly. By the tenth swing, though, Joe Daly was shaking his head. "Your head's flying loose, kid," he rasped. "Hold your hands a bit higher and swing the bat level with the ground."

Eddie watched Tom slowly turn red in the face as he tried to follow the man's instructions. But he was trying to think of too many things at the same time. His concentration fell apart. Tom's T-shirt was soaked with sweat by the time Daly called a halt.

"OK, OK," he said. "I'm not here to waste my time or yours. You need a couple of summers in American Legion ball, Bluth. And a lot of time in the cage here to groove your swing."

"But don't give up," Daly added. "I liked your glove when I watched you. Work with your hitting. Someday it might be worth it to you."

Tom stepped out of the batter's box, trying to hide his disappointment. "I should've let you pinch-hit for me," he muttered to Eddie. He was trying to smile.

"Yeah, that would have gotten it done," John Rivard said.

"Why is that?" Daly asked.

"Eddie's a hitter," Tom said.

"Like to take a few cuts yourself?" Eddie's father asked the scout. "I recall that you hung on in the big leagues for 15 years. Mostly by swinging the bat. They always said you could roll out of bed on New Year's morning and get two hits in your pajamas."

"That a nice brand of snake oil you're peddling," Daly said easily. "You almost sound like a guy trying to set me up for something."

2

Tom Bluth offered Daly his bat. He took it, but he kept watching John Rivard's blank expression. Daly took a couple of quick swings. "OK, don't mind if I do," he said. He placed the bat between his knees while he removed his jacket. Then he turned around and stared at Eddie's father again. "Why do I get the feeling I'm being hustled?"

"Just your suspicious nature," Rivard suggested. "Actually, I was ready to bet you that you couldn't outhit my kid here."

"Ahhh, here it comes," Daly observed. "Except that wouldn't be a bet. That would be like taking candy from a baby—your candy."

"Twenty swings apiece," Eddie's father said. "Make it easy on yourself."

"You're serious?" Daly asked. John Rivard nodded. "For 50 bucks, then," Daly said. He stepped into the batter's box. "Crank it up, kid."

Eddie watched with interest as Joe Daly took a half dozen practice swings. The scout had a big, looping swing, but he hit the practice balls hard. "OK," Daly announced. "Let's go."

Eddie casually moved the speed control over to the final notch. The ball came in and blew past Daly. His hard swing was a clean miss. He glared at Eddie, then grinned as he stepped out to let Eddie take his first swing. "That's right kid," he said cheerfully. "Never give yourself the worst of it."

Eddie had been using a 34-inch, 34-ounce bat when he had taken his cuts earlier. Now he changed to a 35-inch bat that weighed 33 ounces. A bigger bat for a bigger hit. The first pitch came in and he rifled it back in a line drive. It landed two-thirds of the way up the canvas behind the machine.

Daly grunted. "Real whippy swing, kid. Maybe I better get down to business here."

Daly took his second cut and slammed the ball into what would have been left center field. He looked satisfied when he stepped out of the cage. Eddie fouled one off. Daly popped one up. Eddie hit what would have been a double down the line.

Between his own swings Daly leaned forward, hands on his bat, watching Eddie swing. "See that?" Daly called to Tom Bluth. "His head doesn't move."

Eddie and Daly took turns in the cage, until John Rivard spoke up. "Halfway," he said. "I got Eddie with five hits. Daly with three."

"You've got it right," Daly agreed. That's a real innocent-looking tiger you've got here."

They took two more swings apiece. Eddie had two more line drive hits, Daly had a hit and a miss. "Are you playing with someone now?" he asked Eddie as he came out of the batter's box again.

Eddie shook his head. "I keep busy here."

Daly spoke again after he had hit two bullets. One of them might have reached the bleachers in a ballpark. Eddie had missed one of his own two swings. "Where'd you play in high school, Eddie? I mean what position?"

"He was our catcher," Tom Bluth responded. "You ought to see him block a plate."

"I hated every minute of it," Eddie said.

Daly frowned. "Playing?"

"Catching."

"So why not switch? First base, maybe?"

Tom Bluth was smiling. "He was a good hit, no field. We used to call him 'Clang.' Like in 'Iron Glove.'"

Daly grunted. He was silent as he and Eddie completed their 20 swings. "I've got Eddie with 11, Daly 8," John Rivard said.

"Correct," Daly said. He tossed his bat aside and reached for Eddie's. He swung it several times. "A little light," he commented. "For shoulders like yours."

"I move up in weight with a curveball pitcher," Eddie said.

"You've been doing this for a couple of hours a day?" Daly asked. Eddie nodded. "For how long?"

"Seven years."

"Seven years!" Daly shook his head. "Never play the other man's game," he advised himself.

"Except it's your game, too," John Rivard reminded him.

"*Was* my game," Daly said. He was still looking at Eddie. "How old are you?"

"Twenty."

"Do you have a mitt around here?"

Eddie hesitated. He could sense what was coming. "In the locker," he said reluctantly.

"Get it. I want to throw you a few."

Eddie went to get the catcher's mitt. Daly turned to Eddie's father. "It's a wonder he hasn't burned it the way he seems to feel about catching. Why isn't he playing?"

"Tom said it all," John Rivard said. "Eddie never had a position."

"You know what you have here?"

"A hitter."

"A natural hitter," Daly agreed.

Eddie returned with the mitt. Daly led him into the area between the pitching machines and the batting cages. He swung his arm in circles to stretch it out, then paced off 60 feet. "We won't bother measuring it," he said. "OK, kid, here it comes."

Daly threw six pitches, gradually increasing their speed. He could see at once that there was a problem. In contrast to Eddie's smooth style in the batting cage, he was stiff and awkward receiving the pitches.

Daly threw two dozen pitches before he stopped.

"Coffee in the kitchen?" Daly asked abruptly.

"Sure," John Rivard replied.

They started for the house. Joe Daly walked with John Rivard, several steps in front of Eddie and Tom. "Do I get a feeling you're pushing this?" Daly asked.

"That's right," Rivard answered. "Eddie's in a rut here. But he doesn't seem to want to break out of it. He has a nice girlfriend, but he doesn't seem to take much interest even in her. Level with me. Could he make it in pro ball?"

"I'll bring a live pitcher around tomorrow to double-check his hitting," Daly said. "But as far as I'm concerned, he can hit in Double-A right now. All the minor leagues have designated hitters. I think the big question might be his attitude.

"You leave that to me," Eddie's father said confidently.

They entered the kitchen. Daly and Eddie washed up at the sink while John Rivard made the coffee. Tom Bluth struggled to hold down his growing excitement. Was he going to witness an offer to play professional baseball? His own disappointment was forgotten.

"You're already too good a hitter for Class-A ball," Daly said to Eddie when they were all seated. "I can get you top dollar for a balance-of-the-season contract with the Pittsfield Indians. That's the Cubs' Eastern League Double-A club."

Eddie sat in silence.

"What's top dollar?" John Rivard asked.

"Well, let's see. We've lost April, plus you missed spring training. Say $16,000."

"I'm doing as well as that working here," Eddie objected.

"But what's your future here? Can you double your salary? Triple it?"

"I think you ought to try it, Eddie," John Rivard said. There was an urgent note in his voice. "If you don't, you'll always wonder if you could have made it. Tom here can help me run things while you're gone. And he'll get the batting practice he needs while he's doing it."

Eddie opened his mouth, then closed it. Finally, he said, "The bottom line, Mr. Daly, is that the Cubs are in the wrong league. They don't use a designated hitter."

Daly blinked. "Wait, now, we're already talking about the majors? Give it a try with Pittsfield. I could tell you a hundred different ways the thing could go while you're moving up. Do you have any doubts about moving up, Eddie?"

"Not as a hitter," Eddie said quietly.

"So go with the flow." Daly rose to his feet. "I'll be back in the morning with a pitcher and a contract."

3

Joe Daly sat in a first-row seat behind the Pittsfield Indians dugout. He watched as Eddie Rivard came up to the plate for his first at bat as a professional. He was the Indians' designated hitter. As DH, he was batting third, because of what the Indians' manager had seen in batting practice.

The opposing pitcher was young and he was already throwing wild in the first inning. He threw two wide pitches to Eddie, and then he tried to come inside with a fastball. Eddie took his usual long stride. The crack of the bat sent the third baseman leaping high. The ball shot a foot above his outstretched glove.

Watching the flight of the ball, Daly noted that it went straight in a line as it headed for the outfield. It hit the fence two-thirds of the way up and bounced back past the retreating left fielder. Eddie was standing on third when the ball came back to the infield.

Joe Daly relaxed in his seat, smiling. The train was on schedule. He jotted a few lines in his notebook about other players while he waited for Eddie's next turn at bat. When he came up in the fourth inning, Eddie hit a frozen rope to center for a single.

Daly leaned forward in his seat when Eddie had another turn in the seventh. There were runners on first and second and none out. The third baseman had moved back three feet, Daly noted. Eddie's first-inning rocket had told the man something.

Eddie fouled off a pitch. Even though the next one was off the plate outside, he managed to pull it to the second baseman. He was thrown out, but the runners moved up. Daly nodded in approval. Eddie had moved the runners along.

In the ninth, Eddie hit a high drive that the center fielder caught after a long run. Daly went down on the field after the game. He singled out the Indians' veteran first baseman with whom he had played in the majors for a while.

"Well?" Daly challenged. "What about my boy?"

The first baseman, Johnny Cooney, said with a smile, "I think he's got it, Joe. Notice the way the third baseman backed up after the kid's triple? Eddie's a natural left-handed late swinger."

"I didn't realize how late his swing was when I saw him against the pitching machine," Daly admitted.

"He just about hit that triple out of the catcher's glove," Cooney said. "I already told our pitching staff not to throw slow stuff to the kid. I don't want him getting all the way around on it and ramming it down the line to first. All us elderly first basemen have to be careful, you know."

Daly laughed and said, "See you, Johnny."

"Right, Joe. I think you did the team a favor."

Daly climbed through the grandstand to the club office on the second level. "Let me talk to the Chief, Edna, OK?" he said to the woman behind the first desk. The

"Chief" was the Cubs' owner, William Graves. Daly went into the manager's office to wait for Edna to put the call through.

"Two hits, Chief, one a triple," Daly said when Graves came on the line. "And he moved two men up in a no-out situation. Plus, his last time up he ran the center fielder across two county lines to catch up with his air-to-air missile."

"Do I sense a note of enthusiasm, Joe?" Graves asked.

"You do, Chief," Daly said. "You do."

"So what are we going to do with him?"

"Lefferts is going to work him behind the plate every day. He'll work out in the bullpen and during batting practice. And we'll hope."

"Your report said we'll need some luck."

"Right. But he's a once-in-20-years hitter, Chief. I'm betting right now that you'll move him up to Iowa by June." Iowa was the Cubs' Triple-A farm club.

"As raw as he is? That would be asking a lot, Joe."

"I believe it can happen, Chief. And you will, too."

Daly left the office and went down to the clubhouse to take Eddie to dinner. "It was a nice start, Eddie," he said. "But you've got to set your teeth now. Jim Lefferts is going to work your tail off behind the plate. You've got to bear down. You've got to *work*. Forget that you don't like it. You've got to *do* it."

"I can do it," Eddie said. "I just wish I could catch as well as I can hit."

A week later the manager of his rooming house handed Eddie a note when he came downstairs to leave for the ballpark. The note said: "I'm back on the road looking for another one like you. Work! You can make it. Joe Daly."

Eddie was surprised at the sense of loss that he felt. In the short time he had known him, Joe Daly had really propped him up. Now Eddie would have to do it by himself.

Eddie rode to the park every day with five other players. All the riders chipped in weekly for gas. At the park, Eddie caught batting practice, which wasn't too bad. The pitches were usually around the plate. As he caught he found himself studying the swings of the other players.

What Eddie didn't like were the catching drills in the bullpen. First, he warmed up any pitcher who wanted to stretch out his arm. Then he warmed up that night's starting pitcher. Next he worked on the drills that Manager Lefferts had set up. Eddie handled 20 fastballs, then 20 curves, then 20 pitchouts. Then he made 20 throws to first on bunts. And he made 20 more to second for imaginary base stealers. Finally, he went through the whole routine again.

The drill Eddie *really* hated, though, was when the pitchers sat down and an extra outfielder was brought in. The man was instructed to throw at Eddie's ankles. The drill was supposed to give Eddie practice at fielding throws to the plate from the outfield. The outfielder threw a ball that naturally sailed, and that kept Eddie lunging for the ball. The outfielder never knew where it was going, and Eddie didn't, either. His ankles were nipped frequently by balls he missed.

Compared to that, batting as DH was like a walk in the park. It was a rare night when Eddie didn't get at least two hits. Even his outs were impressive. When he laid the bat on the ball, the ball really jumped.

Night after night he studied the opposing pitchers. They had a wide variety of pitching styles. He had noticed right away that the Indians' position players were all young guys like himself. Except for the pitchers. Half of them were guys who had once made it to the big leagues and were now on their way back down. Pitchers seemed to hang on longer.

Eddie finally asked Johnny Cooney about it. "It makes a certain amount of sense," Cooney explained. "Usually when a position player loses it, he packs it in. It may be due to injuries. Or it may be that the legs are gone, or the batting eye is gone, or whatever. But once they go down, they seldom work their way back.

"Pitchers are different, though. No one knows why a pitcher wins, anyway. It's a matter of rhythm. But often it's even more a matter of confidence. Sometimes pitchers lose both from year to year. Sometimes between the start and finish of a season. They can't get anyone out. But every pitcher who makes it to the big leagues has a winning groove. He may not be able to stay in it consistently over a period of years. Only the Hall of Famers do that. But he still has that groove. If he can find it again down here, he has a chance of being picked up again by a big-league team. They know he had it once."

It was on June 14th that Manager Jim Lefferts received a phone call from the Chief. We're thinking of moving Rivard up to Iowa," the Chief said. "I know he's hitting. Daly says he'll do that till they throw dirt over him. But do you think his catching has improved?"

Lefferts hesitated. "He's worked at it, Chief. Worked hard. But Triple-A ball? It's strange how a kid who's so comfortable hitting at the plate can look so awkward catching behind it. But it does seem to me he's doing much better. I hope it's not because I'm just getting used to watching him. You want him right away?"

"The organization can't ignore his bat," the Chief explained.

"We're sure going to miss it here," Lefferts sighed.

4

Eddie reported to the Iowa front office and was introduced to his new manager, Bill Schultz. "We know you'll take this league apart with your bat, too," Schultz said. He could see that Eddie was nervous, so he made his voice soothing.

"And my catching, too?" Eddie asked. "I don't feel like I'm improving, and I don't like it." He had to clamp down on himself to keep the nervousness he felt from showing too much.

"Lefferts said you're getting better," Schultz replied.

Eddie shook his head doubtfully.

That night he was the DH in the Iowa lineup. His second time at bat the opposing pitcher threw him a slow curve. Eddie began his swing and his eyes caught up with the slowness of the pitch. He adjusted his stroke as the ball finally made it over the plate.

The bat met the ball and the result was a screamer hit directly at the first baseman. The man did a tap dance to get out of the way of the rocket Eddie had blasted at him. The ball landed in the right field corner and Eddie made second easily.

Manager Schultz sat down beside him when Iowa took the field. "I had a message from the Chief concerning you," Schultz said. "I'm going to put you into games to catch an inning or two."

Eddie wondered if the fear showed on his face. Go in and catch in a real game? He wasn't ready. But if Schultz thought he was . . .

Eddie couldn't sit still. He grabbed his bat and walked down to the end of the dugout. He stood there and practiced his swing. He knew he was safe for that night because the DH can't replace a position player.

The next night, though, someone else was the DH. Eddie sat on the bench until Manager Schultz made a pitching change in the seventh inning. He put Eddie in at the same time to catch for the new pitcher. Eddie wondered if everyone could see the tight-looking expression he wore behind his mask.

He warmed up the relief pitcher. When the final warm-up pitch reached the plate, Eddie straightened up and threw to second. He was grabbing for the ball almost before it left his fingertips, but it was no use. There was a base runner on third, and when the throw went through, the surprised runner came in to score. Eddie had forgotten there was no throw to second except at the beginning of an inning. The ball was in play when the umpire stepped in behind the catcher.

Eddie stared straight up into the night sky. He had to resist a powerful urge to rip off his mask and walk off the field. He pounded his mitt and crouched down for the first pitch. One of the coaches was calling the pitches from the bench.

Eddie got through the remainder of the game without any more mental mistakes. Hitting in the catcher's spot, he rifled a drive to the left-field fence and one to right center. He drove in three runs and felt a bit better about the game.

The next night he was put in to catch again. It was the sixth inning. The game was proceeding smoothly—Iowa had a big lead—until the ninth. Then Eddie stood at the plate and watched as a base runner tried to score from second on a single.

Eddie took the good throw from the outfield. He met the runner a step or two up the third-base line. Eddie never even let the would-be scorer reach the plate. He sent the sliding runner sideways with a solid block that pushed him halfway toward the backstop. Even during his high school days Eddie had somehow known the correct angle to get on a sliding base runner.

Bill Schultz reported to the Chief the following week. "He'll pick it up," he said. "He has some good instincts. He just hasn't spent enough time behind the dish. Plus it's plain he's never liked it."

There was a short silence at the other end of the line. "We might bring him up," the Chief said. "In August."

"Why?" Schultz demanded. He didn't want to lose Eddie's bat from his lineup. "You'll only get one at bat a day out of him as a pinch hitter."

"We're not hitting as much as we need to," the Chief said. "As you can see by the box scores. If we can score a few runs, we've got a chance to win our division."

"On one at bat a day from Rivard?" Schultz asked, trying to sound scornful.

"Keep working him behind the plate," the Chief said.

One night early in August, Eddie was in the clubhouse pulling on his shirt. He was listening to a radio announcer giving the big-league scores. Half a dozen players were standing around listening for the Cubs' score. The Cubs had won that afternoon, 3-1. But then the announcer said, "Tito Corbin, the Cubs' first string catcher, broke his leg today in a home-plate collision."

"Oh, no, Tito was carrying them, too," one of the veterans said. "They'll have to pick up a catcher." He was looking at Eddie. "No offense, kid, but you're not ready."

Eddie didn't disagree. Still, he felt quite a bit different about it than when he had first arrived in Iowa. He didn't feel exactly confident yet. But he was beginning to feel more comfortable. His catching was improving. He began to do some things without having to think about them. And he felt *very* good about his hitting. He had hit .388 during his time with Pittsfield and was now batting .341 with Iowa.

The next morning, first thing as usual, Eddie turned to the sports pages. The Cubs had traded for Carlos Fuentes, a catcher who had been with Toronto in the American League. Eddie knew that Fuentes was great at handling pitchers. But he wasn't much of a hitter.

When he got to the ballpark, Eddie was told to report to manager Schultz's office. The manager did not look happy at all. For a moment Eddie became worried. Then Schultz sighed and began to smile a little. "You're headed for the Windy City, kid," he said.

It took Eddie a few seconds to remember that the Windy City was Chicago's nickname. He tried to hide his shock— and his excitement.

"Even after they traded for Fuentes?" he asked.

"The Chief insists the Cubs need hitting," Schultz said. "Good luck, Eddie.

I hate to lose you. Don't press. Let it come naturally."

Eddie packed his bags, said good-bye to his teammates, and headed for the train station.

The next afternoon the Cubs held a press conference to announce Eddie's arrival. Moon Roberts, the Cubs' manager, sat beside Eddie who looked nervously at the several reporters gathered in front of him.

Eddie tried to handle it coolly. He responded quietly to the first few questions. Then at one point he said, "Ask me about hitting, guys. I'm not a ballplayer yet."

When the questions focused on his hitting, Eddie answered in his usual no-nonsense style. But the questioning swung back around to catching. Eddie tried to keep his good humor, but his answers became more defensive. Finally he held up his hand. "Look," he said. "I made it as a hitter. And I'll make it as a catcher. It just may take a little time."

With that statement, the press conference ended. "You handled that well," Moon Roberts said as the reporters and a few TV people departed. "Come on, the Chief's waiting to meet you. He's been watching from next door."

Eddie was to learn that William Graves was almost always watching from next door. Graves didn't want any attention from the press. He shook hands with Eddie warmly. "Welcome to the Cubs," he said in a deep voice.

"Glad to be here," Eddie replied.

"Did you tell him, Moon?" the Chief asked.

"Not yet." Roberts turned to Eddie. "Ralph Moody has a sore shoulder. We couldn't let it out before the Fuentes trade. If we had, we would have had to give up even more to get him."

"So now it's Fuentes," Eddie said slowly.

"And you."

Eddie was stunned. He opened his mouth to speak and then closed it again. The Chief spoke before Eddie could. "We wouldn't want you to think we were overloading you," he said, his voice now sounding mellow. "It's just that the program here now says that anytime we need a pinch hit for Fuentes—it will be Rivard."

"The hitting doesn't worry me," Eddie said after a few seconds' silence. "But getting behind the plate—"

"We won't be expecting Johnny Bench," Roberts said.

"Not at first," the Chief added. He was smiling.

"We've put you up in a motel for now. Harry Edwards will take you there. Then you can look around for a place yourself," Roberts said.

The Chief picked up his phone and almost immediately a young man walked into the office. He was introduced to Eddie and the two left the room. Roberts and the Chief looked at each other after the door had closed.

"Well?" the Chief said.

"It's a load to drop on a kid," Roberts said. "I know, I know," he said when he saw that the Chief was going to interrupt him. "We've got a chance to win the division. And we've got to make do with what we have. I just hope we don't ruin him by expecting too much."

"He doesn't strike me as the type of young fellow who can be ruined easily," the Chief said. He paused for a moment.

"I slipped down to Iowa and watched him for a couple of nights. I didn't go near anyone in the organization. I just sat in the stands and watched him."

The corners of Roberts's mouth moved upward. "And?" he said.

"I think my blood pressure went down 30 points."

"That's what Daly said," Roberts agreed. "And Lefferts. Well, let's cross our fingers."

CHAPTER

5

Eddie woke in the morning surprised that he had slept so well. He had expected to have a restless night. He couldn't get out of his mind the big responsibility he would have when he had to catch for the Cubs.

He knew he had come a long way from Pittsfield. But he still had concerns. Most of his worries centered around his throwing. He'd had no spring training. And the first month in Pittsfield his arm had ached all the time. It wasn't anything serious. It was just a sore arm caused by all the extra throwing he'd done.

By the time he joined the Iowa team his arm had strengthened quite a bit, although it was still tender at times. It had improved even more while he was with Iowa, but it was still no cannon. And with big-league players running the bases to test him . . .

Within a week Eddie was feeling comfortable with his new teammates. The players had watched him in the batting cage and behind the plate when he relieved Fuentes. The opinion in the locker room was that Eddie could help the team. Ballplayers in a pennant race will accept help from any source.

One day around noon, the phone rang in William Graves's office. It was Moon Roberts calling from the dugout. "Walk out to your second-deck box, Chief," Roberts said. "I want you to see this."

Graves went out to the box and sat down. He picked up the phone there and once again was connected to Roberts in the dugout. "OK," Graves announced. "What am I supposed to be watching?"

"The batting cage," Roberts answered.

The batting practice cage had just been wheeled into position at home plate. Eddie Rivard was eagerly standing beside the cage, bat in hand. He jumped into the cage even before the pitcher pulled the screen across the front of the mound. On the ground piled next to the cage were

Eddie's chest protector, shin guards, mask, and mitt.

Eddie began straightening out the pitches coming in to the plate. Sharp grounders, line drives, and whistling extra-base hits rocketed all around the ballpark. Players out on the field stopped what they were doing to watch.

"I go back a way, Chief," Roberts said softly into the phone. "But I don't remember seeing anyone hit it so often or hit it so hard."

"Eddie looks like a pure hitter," the Chief agreed.

After he had his swings, Eddie ran out of the cage and began to put on his gear.

"Catch you later, Moon," the Chief said. "The show's over."

"It's just starting," Roberts said. "Hold on."

Eddie settled into his catcher's crouch as the Cub players each took a turn in the cage. They used the starting lineup order for their first cuts. Then the bench players hit, and finally the pitchers.

Eddie kept up a constant stream of chatter as he hustled his teammates along. "Hit, hit, hit!" he chirped whenever a player showed signs of a passing up a pitch. And if a player was ten seconds late getting into the cage, Eddie was up at bat again, equipment and all, taking an extra cut or two. Bang! would go another liner off a wall of the bullpen gate.

"I hope they don't think he's a pain," the Chief said. There was a note of worry in his voice.

"Naah," Roberts said. "They think he's funny. Fitzie says he's the same way in the bullpen, too. Always go, go, go. He's always got someone up throwing to him. Fitzie says he pitches to the kid himself to save the staff arms."

"Why doesn't Fitzie run Eddie around the outfield ten laps a day? That would take some of the steam out of him," the Chief commented.

"Hey, when you're in a pennant race, steam is what you want. Besides, the guys are starting to think Eddie is a good luck charm. We were three games out when he got here. Now it's only half a game."

With that the Chief hung up the phone. But he remained in his box until batting practice ended.

Soon Moon Roberts began moving Eddie in behind the plate as early as the fifth or sixth inning. He did it even when there was no need to hit for Fuentes. "Crash course for the kid," Roberts explained one day to his third-base coach. "Got to get him ready for the Series."

"The Series!" the coach exclaimed. "Don't jinx us, Moon. First let's win the division. And the league."

"It's in the bag," Roberts replied. "This team is up and running. I've seen it happen before. Something clicks, and away they go. We'll breeze to the division and then take the pennant. The Yankees will be a different story, though. They're a better ball club than we are."

The first ten days of September made Roberts looks like a genius. The Cubs won two out of every three games, and they stretched out to a three-game lead. Eddie was still putting new dents in the outfield walls. "The only thing Eddie can't contribute is experience," the Chief said to Roberts one morning.

Roberts nodded. "Yeah, and he's surrounded by that. He gives them zip and they give him cool. It's a great combination."

Leading by five games, the Cubs came down to the final week of the season. One more game would give them the division title. The players went out on the field that afternoon feeling very confident. But by the fifth inning they were trailing 4-1.

Their opponents, the Reds, put two men on in the top of the sixth. Moon Roberts came out to change pitchers for the second time. There were runners on second and third with one out. Just before the two-and-two pitch came in to the hitter, a Cub coach jumped up on the dugout step and waved the left fielder closer to the foul line.

The fielder was in motion when the pitch arrived at the plate. The batter swung and nubbed the ball off the end of his bat. The ball popped over the third baseman's head. Normally there would have been no one near it. But now the left fielder was moving directly toward it.

The runner on third started casually toward the plate. The runner on second was sprinting toward third. He flew around the bag and started toward home plate, only a few feet behind the lead runner.

The Cub left fielder dashed toward the ball and grabbed it on the first bounce. He fired it in a line to the plate. Eddie stood still, his hands at his sides. At the last moment he reached out for the ball and tagged the startled base runners, one-two. On a base hit two runners had been tagged out at the plate. The inning was over.

"Did you see that?" Moon Roberts shouted. "Did you see the way he decoyed those two? That's baseball instinct. You can spend years in this business and not be able to teach that."

The Cubs rushed in from the field cheering. The first five batters in their half of the inning reached base safely, and two of them came in to score. Then Eddie cleared the bases with a triple. The Cubs were leading, 6-4. They added another run in the eighth, and won, 7-4.

The win gave them the division title. The season ended the following Sunday and the league championship series began on Tuesday. The Cubs were playing the Dodgers in Los Angeles for the first two games. The Cubs got off to a great start, winning the first game, 5-2, and the second, 7-4.

Eddie hadn't had a base hit in either game, although he had hit several balls hard. He had also started both games. "It's the catching that's affecting my hitting," Eddie explained to a coach during the flight back to Chicago. "I'm not making excuses, and I'm not complaining. It's a fact, that's all."

"Look, when the bench calls the signals for the pitcher, I have to know them, too. I have to *see* them. With men on base I can't be looking for a fastball when a curve is coming. I have to *know*, and that's where my concentration is going. But I'll catch up to the Dodger pitchers."

The third game was played on Friday after the travel-day layoff. Eddie had four of the Cubs' total of six hits, and the Cubs won, 2-1. They had had three very well-pitched ball games. "One to go! One to go!" was the only thing that could be heard in the roaring clubhouse afterward.

6

On Saturday afternoon the Dodgers caught up with the Cub pitching. The Cub outfielders wore out their arms returning hard-hit balls to the infield. Eddie had two hits, but the rest of the Cubs had only two more. The Cubs lost, 8-0.

The clubhouse was quieter, but there was no real loss of confidence. They had one more shot at the Dodgers right in the Cub ballpark. "We'll get them tomorrow," Moon Roberts declared. Everybody just dig in and do his thing tomorrow. That'll take care of business."

By the end of the fourth inning of the next game, the Cubs were leading, 6-2. The fans were cheering wildly. Behind the plate Eddie kept waiting for an unpleasant surprise or two. But the game rolled along, all downhill for the Dodgers. The final score was 9-3. Eddie had three more hits and drove in two runs.

The clubhouse was a lot quieter than Eddie imagined a pennant-winning one would be. It was as though everyone were already thinking about the upcoming World Series with the Yankees. That would be for all the marbles.

Moon Roberts was busy scheduling clubhouse meetings before the start of the Series. He told everyone who would listen that the Yankees were going to be a different story than the Dodgers. Eddie agreed. The Yankee lineup was solid.

Eddie was surprised when he arrived at the first clubhouse meeting. Scout Joe Daly was sitting there with Moon Roberts and his coaches. Daly grinned across the room at Eddie, and Eddie waved.

"We've got a lot of ground to cover here," Roberts began right away. "Now let's listen to a man who has seen better than half the players in the Yankee system come up through the minors. Joe Daly, you have the floor."

Daly accepted a Yankee lineup card, but referred constantly to his own battered-looking notebook. He described what he knew about the strengths and the weaknesses of the opposing players. "But remember," Daly continued when he had completed his talk, "I saw them on the way up. If they hadn't improved, they wouldn't be here. So don't take anyone for granted."

Daly crossed the room to speak to Eddie when the meeting broke up. "Dinner together?" he asked. "On me?"

"Sure, but why on you?"

"For making me look good for signing you," Daly said bluntly.

Eddie smiled. "Maybe so, but I owe you a lot, too."

They caught a cab to one of Daly's favorite restaurants. "You can cut the steak here with your fingernail," Daly promised Eddie. When the meal came, they both fell silent until they had satisfied the first edge of their hunger.

Daly leaned back in his chair. "Do you have any idea how different you look?" he asked Eddie. "How different you sound?"

"In what way?" Eddie asked.

Daly waved his fork. "You're much more outgoing. There's a take-charge attitude that wasn't there before. You don't sound like the man I listened to in Pittsfield."

Eddie laughed. "If I hadn't signed that contract with you, I'd have packed it up and gone back to the pitching machines. But you kept telling me I could make it."

"That's right. What are you going to do this winter? You ought to go down to the Dominican League and polish your game."

"Roberts has already been on me about that. But not right away. First I've got some home cooking to catch up with. And a girl . . . ," his voice faded for a moment. "It's lonely up here sometimes, even when the team is at home. It would be nice to have someone to go out with after the game, other than teammates. Help me get my mind off baseball."

"It would do you good," Daly agreed. "Settle you down. Although I must say you're a lot more settled down than most kids your age."

Their talk drifted to the Series and the Yankees.

The Yankees won the first two games of the Series in New York. They won them easily. Professionally. There was no glitter to their performance. They simply went out on the field and got the job done.

During both games they led all the way from the early innings.

"If we could only get out of the gate ahead of them," Moon Roberts said during the plane ride back to Chicago. "Make them press a little. Make them sweat."

Eddie listened silently. He'd had a hit in each game. But they weren't the ringing smashes the Cubs were used to seeing from him. The Yankees were pitching Eddie tight, right in on his hands. It took away the long stride he usually used to snap the bat around on the ball. He wasn't too concerned. But he had already promised himself that he would make some changes when they played at Wrigley Field.

The Yankees got out in front again in the third game. Eddie drove in a run in the second inning with a long double. But the Cubs were playing catch-up again. Eddie had widened his stance a bit. That way he got a better look at the ball as it came in over his right shoulder.

Eddie came up next in the fifth with two men on. He hit a bullet to left center. The two Cub runners scored. But the ball rebounded so sharply from the wall that

Eddie found it waiting for him as he slid into second base. He was furious at himself for having chopped off a promising rally.

The Cubs had taken a one-run lead, and Moon Roberts used four pitchers to hold that slender margin. Hope bloomed in the Cubs dugout. They'd show those Yankees they weren't going to have things their own way every game.

However, the Yankees came out the next day and blitzed the Cubs. The game was all but over by the sixth inning. Then the Cubs came back in the fifth game, the one they had to win to stay alive. They clawed and scratched and stumbled their way to a one-run win. And everyone packed up and flew back to New York.

In the sixth game Eddie singled to left his first time up. It would have been a double except that the ball hit the third-base bag. The Yankee third baseman hadn't figured Eddie for the late swinger that he was. Your own league always knew you better.

The Cubs were retired without scoring, and the Yankees scored two in their half of the first. They scored three more in the second and another three in the fourth. Moon Roberts went to the mound twice to change pitchers, but nothing seemed to help.

Eddie drove in a run in the fifth with a sacrifice fly and the Cubs scored twice more in the same inning. But that was their last gasp. They were shut down the rest of the way. The final score was 8-3.

Eddie made the last out of the game. He'd smacked a long screamer that the center fielder pulled down as he crashed into the padded fence. The Cubs retreated silently to their dugout.

"Well, we made them work for it," someone said in the clubhouse.

"Yeah, we'll get them next year," another player chimed in.

The Chief and Moon Roberts circled the room, clapping the disappointed players on the shoulder.

"We've got to get a couple of right-handed bats into the lineup next season," Eddie overheard the Chief saying to the manager. "Let's talk about it in the morning."

So next season had already begun, Eddie thought. He looked back in wonder at his own rookie season. Perhaps his biggest boost was being accepted by the Cub players. Next year it was going to be a sweet deal to go all the way with them. He'd never even dreamed of such a thing in Pittsfield.

He unbuttoned his uniform and headed for the showers.

Casey's Claw

David St. Vincent

1

It was late in the game. The Tigers were down by two goals and heading for their sixth straight loss. They'd played well enough to keep it close, but they were sagging badly in the later stages of the game. Their opponents, the Stars, were starting to skate them into the ice.

For Tiger captain Bobby Drake, it was discouraging. The ex-NHL defenseman was playing some of the best hockey of his career. But it wasn't enough to turn his team around. What the Tigers really needed was some youth. They were the oldest team in minor-league pro hockey, and it showed.

Bobby was 35 years old. That made him part of the problem, whether he was playing well or not. That idea pushed him on, made his skates bite a little deeper into the ice. He had to make something happen.

Bobby knew that sooner or later he would get a break. When it came, he would have to make the most of it.

The break came when there were only five minutes left in the game. Bobby was gambling a bit, moving up from the defense. A bad pass by the Stars bounced off his leg and landed in front of him. He picked up the puck at his own line, and for a moment he was in the clear.

But the goal was a long way off, and 15 years as a pro had taken something out of Bobby's legs. By the time he struggled across the center, both Star defensemen were back and waiting for him. The closest, a tall kid with a droopy mustache, looked up at him and smiled.

Bobby slowed down and looked for help. But no one was in position for a pass. The two Star defenders had Bobby lined up and were moving in for the hit. Both were smiling now.

There was only one thing for Bobby to do—try to split the defense. Bobby waited as the defenders came together. Then he dug in a skate and tried to skate between them.

It almost worked. His upper body made it through. But a stick caught between his knees and he spilled forward. He crashed to the ice just as the linesman blew the whistle for an offside call.

Some of the Tigers screamed for a penalty, but the ref was having none of it. The kid with the droopy mustache skated over and picked up the stick from between Bobby's legs.

"You'll never get back to the bigs playing like that, pop," he said with a lopsided grin.

Bobby looked up and laughed. "I'm 35," he said. "I've given up on waiting for the phone to ring."

As the kid skated away, Bobby took note of the big number "4" on his back. Number Four would do well to keep an eye out for him in the future.

The referee skated by as Bobby was getting to his feet. "Shake it off, Drake, or else get to the bench," he growled. "We've got a game to finish here."

"Easy, Henry," Bobby said. "I'm fine. Give me a minute or two to skate the cobwebs out. OK?"

Henry scowled. "Make it snappy then."

Bobby skated the length of the ice in a lazy curl. In the Tigers' net, Gordie Stone was sweeping "snow" out of the crease with his goal stick. He grinned up through his mask as Bobby coasted up beside him.

"You OK, Captain?" Gordie asked.

"Never felt better," Bobby lied. "Think you can hold them off for the rest of the game?"

Gordie shrugged. "Don't see why not," he said. "With a little help from my friends, of course. Uh-oh, Bobby, here comes Malone."

Bobby turned. Buck Malone was puffing toward him from the bench. Malone was sweating, and his stringy hair hung down from his helmet in damp ropes. Malone was the scarred veteran of many hockey wars. He was the closest thing to a "policeman" that the Tigers had.

"I saw that," Malone yelled in his raspy voice. "That guy pitchforked you pretty good."

"It was an accident, Malone," Bobby said.

Malone ground to a stop, laughing. "Sure. An accident." He flashed a toothless grin.

"Anyway, you don't have to worry about him. I'm going to get even for us."

"Don't bother," Bobby said. "I fight my own battles."

"Nobody says you don't, Bobby. I'm just telling you."

Gordie looked up from the net. "Better not, Malone," he said. "You haven't won a fight in five years. Face it, you're just as old and worn-out as the rest of us."

"Shut up," Malone told him. "Bobby, we've got to shake things up a bit. Maybe a scrap right now is what we need to get things turned our way."

Bobby looked at him. "Your timing is lousy, Malone. This game is over. A penalty right now would seal it."

Malone's eyes narrowed. "I'm not asking you for permission, Bobby. I'm telling you. Understand?"

"Why mention it at all, then?"

Malone shook his head. "You're wearing Casey's claw, aren't you? I figured you had a right to know."

Malone skated away. Bobby followed him back to the face-off circle, watching him carefully. A lot of voices lately had been saying that Malone was bad for the team. And Bobby wondered if they might be right.

The Stars won the face-off cleanly, and the puck was swept around on the boards for Number Four. The gangly kid picked it up in full stride, and started to bring it out over the line. Suddenly, Bobby saw Malone taking a run at the kid from the blind side.

There was no way Number Four could have seen Malone coming. His eyes were up the ice, looking to make a pass. Malone had the angle on him and was closing in like a freight train.

Somehow, the kid must have sensed him. At the last second, he looked up. When he saw Malone, his mustache seemed to stand up on end. He dug his skates in, trying to stop, trying to avoid the check. He managed to dodge the worst of it. But Malone still got a big enough piece of him to spill both players to the ice.

As they slid into the boards, Number Four brought up his gloved fist and pushed it angrily into Malone's face. Malone threw off his gloves and went at him. The fight was on.

Bobby arrived with a knot of other players, all trying to crowd in on the action. The referee waved them back and told them to keep their distance.

"Let them go, guys!" Henry was yelling. "We have a fair fight here, so just let them go until they get tired. Keep out of it, or you're through for the night."

From where Bobby stood, the fight didn't look fair at all. The kid with the mustache was ten years younger and 20 pounds heavier, and Malone was taking quite a beating. When the linesman finally pried them apart, Malone was sporting a thick lip and a cut over his left eye.

Malone skated past Bobby on his way to the penalty box. "I told you I'd get him," Malone said.

Bobby said nothing. There was really nothing to say.

Malone was given the extra penalty, two minutes for charging. He squawked a bit about it, but it was a good call. It also took the last bit of fight out of the Tigers.

The Stars scored another goal with the one-man advantage, then played out the last few minutes in command. The final score was Stars 4, Tigers 1.

CHAPTER

2

After the game, the dressing room was very quiet. The players slumped on their benches and folding chairs and tried to avoid each other's eyes. They looked beaten, both in body and in spirit.

Bill Topay, the Tiger coach, stuck his head in for a peek. Then he quickly retreated down the hallway to his office. Bobby Drake dressed in a hurry and went down to join him.

In addition to being coach and general manager of the Tigers, Topay owned a local car dealership. He also owned a fair-sized chunk of the Tigers. Topay looked up as Bobby came in. "Nice game," he said. "I think the team is starting to improve."

"You really think so, Coach?" Bobby asked tiredly. He slumped into a chair and took a long, hard look at the coach. Topay was around 50 and slightly built, with an open face and a fondness for three-piece suits. As a hockey man, he was a good car salesman.

"We were in this one for a long time," Topay said. "We might have won if Malone hadn't pulled his stunt."

"We were never in it," Bobby said. "We were outplayed from the beginning."

"That argument won't wash, Bobby. Buck Malone cost us that game, and you know it as well as I do."

"I don't agree. It was over long before that."

"Still protecting him, eh, Bobby?" he asked.

"That's got nothing to do with it," Bobby said.

"He's trouble, Bobby. I'd have gotten rid of him a long time ago if you hadn't stood up for him."

"Malone's all right, Coach. He's a good team player."

"He's a has-been, Bobby. What's worse, he's afraid to admit it. And so are you." Topay looked Bobby in the eye. "You two broke in the same year, didn't you?"

"As a matter of fact, we did. Seventy-one. So what?"

"Look, Bobby, most of the time I take your advice around here. We all know I'm no hockey man, and to be quite frank, I appreciate your help. But I can't trust your judgment as far as Malone is concerned."

"Yeah?" Bobby said. "And why is that, Coach?"

"I don't know, Bobby. Maybe if you admit that Malone is too old, you might have to admit the same thing about yourself."

Bobby stood up. "You think I'm too old? Is that it?"

"Don't get your shirt in a knot. I was making a point, that's all." Topay looked up and smiled. "Listen, I'll need you to handle practice tomorrow, OK? I'm going to be tied up all day."

"Doing what? Selling cars?"

"No, Bobby, This is team business."

"I'll bet."

"If you did, you'd lose," Topay said. "Clyde Borden's in town. We've got a few things to talk about."

"Borden's *here?*" Borden was the assistant general manager of the Tigers' parent club, the guy responsible for the whole farm system. If Borden was in town, a player move or two was in the works. "Did he see the game?"

"I'd imagine so," Topay said. "Unless he was lucky enough to miss his plane."

Topay walked with Bobby back to the dressing room. Most of the players were still there, hanging around, as if they had no other place to go.

"Will you talk to Malone for me?" Topay asked.

Bobby nodded. "I'll do what I can."

Just then the door opened, and Clyde Borden walked in with someone else in tow. Borden was a thin, tall man whose clothes looked as if they'd been slept in. The fellow with him was a dark, unhappy-looking youth, wearing sunglasses and a black leather jacket.

Borden gave them all a toothy grin. "Hi, Bill. Bobby. Say hello to your new teammate, guys."

Players around the dressing room stopped what they were doing and looked up. Bobby and Topay exchanged looks. "OK, Clyde," Topay said. "I give up. Who is he?"

"You mean you don't know?" Borden's grin widened. "Bill, this is the guy who's going to turn your team around. This is Eddie King."

Eddie King looked up and smiled briefly.

Then Borden launched into a summary of Eddie King's short but brilliant career. Bobby edged his way back through the players until someone grabbed his arm.

It was Malone. "Look at that, will you?" Malone hissed. "He's just a punk kid!"

"Impressive stats, though," Bobby hissed back. The kid had been in the NHL for a season and a half, and according to Borden he had played very well.

"But *look* at him, Bobby!"

Bobby looked. Eddie was leaning against the wall, still in his jacket and shades. He was chewing on a wad of gum and looked bored. "I don't envy you wearing that claw, Bobby," Malone said.

Bobby shrugged. "He's supposed to be a good player. Maybe it won't be so bad."

"That's a laugh!" Malone rasped. "Bobby, if the kid is so darn good, why did they send him down?"

"I suppose he's got a few things to learn," Bobby said.

Borden finished his speech, and Bill Topay added a few choice words of his own. Then he called Bobby down front.

"Bobby, Clyde and I have to get going," Topay said. "Introduce Eddie to the guys, will you? Eddie, this is your captain, Bobby Drake. He'll show you around. OK?"

"I was wondering," Eddie said to Bobby, after Borden and Topay had left. "I hear you're the real brains behind this outfit, not the guy in the three-piece suit. Is that true?"

"Stick around," Bobby said. "Maybe you'll find out."

"I doubt it. Are you the same Bobby Drake who used to play for Montreal?"

Bobby smiled. "Yes. It was a long time ago."

"It sure was," Eddie replied. "I thought you would have retired by now. Almost everyone else your age has."

Bobby's smile faded. "Is that a fact?"

Malone got up, growling. "Watch your mouth, kid," he said.

"You're Malone, aren't you?" Eddie asked in a sneering manner. "Are you captain of the goon squad down here—the way you were in the NHL?"

Malone stepped forward, his face red. "Why, you—"

Bobby grabbed Malone by the arm. "Hold it," he said. And then he turned to Eddie. "Go on, kid. You seem to have something you want to say, so say it. We're all listening."

"All right, it's just this. I don't plan on staying down here for very long. So we don't need to be friends. I don't see myself fitting in with this team. And I'm sure you're not interested in *having* me fit in. But we can still help each other out."

"And how's that, Eddie?" Bobby asked coldly.

"I play down here for awhile and show the brass upstairs I've picked up the experience I need. At the same time I help you guys win some games. It sure looks like you can use the help. I know I can make this team look good—because *I'm* good."

"Is that it?" Bobby asked.

"That's all I have to say," Eddie answered.

"Good," Bobby said sharply. "Practice is at ten o'clock tomorrow, Eddie. You be there, and don't be late. Now get out of here."

As King walked out the door, Malone growled. "That nasty little punk!" he rasped. "How can you take that kind of stuff, Bobby?"

"I get lots of practice," he said. "Well, at least we know one thing."

"Yeah? What's that?"

"We know why they sent him down," Bobby said with a frown. "The kid's got a few things to learn, all right."

CHAPTER

3

Eddie King may have come on like a nightmare, but on the ice in practice he turned out to be a dream. He was an excellent skater, quick and tireless and smooth. His shots were heavy, and always on the net. The only flaw Bobby could find in his game was a desire to run around on defense instead of taking the man.

Bobby called him over during the two-on-two drill. "When the guy passes the puck, don't just turn away," Bobby told him. "Get a piece of him, and finish the check. Take the passer out of the play, and you take away the give-and-go."

"I don't have to play an old man's game," Eddie replied. "There's nothing scary about the give-and-go if you've got enough speed to recover."

Bobby glared at him. "Sound defensive hockey isn't just an old man's game, Eddie. It's what wins hockey games."

The kid smiled. "Yeah. But wide-open hockey is better for my stats."

"You don't care if we win, then?"

"I don't care *what* happens to this two-bit team of yours," Eddie snapped. "I'm trying to get back into the NHL. Understand?"

"Yeah, I understand. Thanks for being so frank."

"My pleasure."

"Malone!" Bobby yelled. "Get over here!"

Malone coasted over with his helmet in his hands. "Yeah, Bobby? What's up?"

"Take the kid out there and give him the puck," Bobby said coldly. "Then show him how to finish the check."

Malone grinned. "I'd love to, Bobby. Thanks."

Bobby had the rest of the players stop what they were doing, and they gathered around to watch. Bobby wanted to see how the kid behaved in the spotlight.

Malone waited on the blue line while Eddie started with the puck on the center spot. At the sound of Bobby's whistle, the kid moved in slowly. He took the puck to the right boards to draw Malone in away from the center.

Once Malone was committed, Eddie faked a centering pass and stepped smoothly to the inside. Malone sailed right past him into the boards. The kid walked into the slot and put the puck in the empty net. Some of the players applauded.

"Hey, no fair!" Malone screamed. "He's supposed to *pass!*"

"No one to pass to," the kid laughed. "Try again?"

"You bet your eyes I will," Malone rasped.

They lined up and did it again. This time, Bobby asked Gordie Stone to skate down the inside in position to take a pass.

This time, Eddie King did pass—a perfect strike that Stone took in mid-stride. Malone moved in to finish the check on Eddie.

After the last time, Malone wasn't taking any chances. He maintained good position and closed the kid off slowly, giving up force for accuracy. When he finally collided with Eddie, it was just a gentle bump. But then the kid brought up his arms and rapped Malone solidly in the upper chest.

Malone was jolted back and very nearly lost his balance. He grabbed a handful of Eddie King's jersey for support and barely managed to stay on his feet.

Malone bared his teeth. "You punk!" he growled.

Eddie pushed him again. "Get your hands off me, man!"

Bobby skated between them. "Cut it out, you two," he said. "Let's save the rough stuff for the bad guys, huh?"

"Let me go, Bobby," Malone snarled. "I'm gonna teach this kid here some respect."

"Respect? Don't make me laugh!" Eddie spat on the ice. "You're a cheap goon, Malone. What do you know about respect?"

"That's enough, both of you!" Bobby grabbed Malone by the shirt and pulled him away. "Malone, get out there and run through some three-on-three."

"But, Bobby, I just—"

"*Now*, Malone!" Bobby snapped. "I want to talk to Eddie."

Malone lowered his eyes and skated away. "The guy's crazy, you know," Eddie said.

"Yeah, kid, he's crazy," Bobby said. "He's crazy enough to have a wife and three kids and a mortgage. He knows that he's too old, that any talent he may once have had is gone. But he's crazy enough to keep on playing the game anyway— because he needs it and because he doesn't know anything else."

"The team can't afford to carry him," Eddie whispered. "You must know that."

"The team? Since when did you care about the team, Eddie? I thought you only cared about your stats."

Eddie winced. "At least a few of my goals and assists will help the team. What's Malone got to offer?"

"More than you think," Bobby told him. "He's a team man, Eddie. If we need a punching bag, he'll take a couple on the chin for us. Anything I ask, he'll do."

"He's crazy," Eddie muttered. "But I think I understand him. The guy I really can't figure out is you."

"Me?" Bobby looked at him.

"Yeah. You've been out of the NHL for a few years now, man, and you're not getting any younger. You must know that the chances of you getting called up again are slim? True?"

"True," Bobby agreed. "So what?"

"Well, look at what you're doing. You're hanging on with this joke of a minor-league team. You play with players who can't play, and coach for coaches who can't coach. And all the time you've got to watch out that the crazies don't beat up their own teammates. Why do you bother?"

Bobby reached up to his throat and pulled out the chain and pendant he always wore.

"Do you see this?" he asked

Eddie poked it with a finger. "What is it? Some kind of tooth?"

"It's a claw, Eddie. A tiger's claw. It goes along with the 'C' on my sweater. This is why I bother, Eddie."

"A tiger's claw?"

"It's real, too. Jack Casey picked it up when he was in India. He wore it all the time when he was captain of this team. Did you get to play with Jack in the NHL?"

Eddie nodded. "Yeah, we paired on defense quite a bit," he said. "Jack's a super hockey player and a real leader."

"Jack passed the claw on to me, the day he was called up," Bobby said. "He walked up to me and said, 'I guess you're in charge now, Bobby.' And he handed me the claw."

"I didn't realize Jack was the captain when he played on this team," Eddie said.

"He was a *great* captain," Bobby replied.

Eddie looked thoughtful. He shook his head and said, "Well, I admire Jack a lot. But I think what this team needs is a few young guys who know how to find the net."

"Every team needs a leader," Bobby said. "That's part of what makes it a team."

"I guess what you're doing is important to you—and maybe it is to this team, too. But a guy your age, after the years at the top . . . I still don't understand what you get out of it. And you can't go on much longer, can you?"

Bobby smiled. "I've got a few miles left in me yet," he said. "You just wait and see."

Eddie shrugged his shoulders. "I'd like to skate. OK?"

"Yeah. Go run through the drills and work up a sweat. Oh, and Eddie? Keep away from Malone, if you know what's good for you. Messing with a man's pride is dangerous."

"It's not my style to look for a fight," he replied. "But if he starts something, I'll be ready."

After practice, Bobby cornered Malone in the parking lot and told him to keep away from the kid.

"But, Bobby, I *owe* him one," Malone whined.

"No, you don't," Bobby told him. "The guy you owe is *me*, Malone. They're trying to get rid of you again."

Malone's face fell. "Topay?" he asked.

"Among others."

"Lousy car salesman!' Malone said bitterly. "What does he know about hockey?"

"I can't hold him off forever," Bobby said. "You'd do yourself a real favor by attracting less attention."

"I'll try, Bobby."

"You know what I mean, Malone. No stupid penalties, no fights, no shooting off your mouth. Play it cool."

"I'll do my best. It's not always easy."

"And stay away from the kid, Malone. If anything happens to Eddie, I'm holding you responsible."

"I'll do what I can, Bobby," Malone said. "I just hope he's got the brains to stay out of my way."

Bobby was hoping the same thing. He had all the makings of a first-class feud on his hands. And he wondered if he'd be able to handle it.

4

Over the next two weeks, the Tigers surprised everyone by winning four of their next five games.

The main reason for this turnabout was the brilliant play of Eddie King. The kid scored an amazing total of eight goals in five games. He became an instant hero. He was the darling of the local press and the press sold him to the fans. He was the Kid Phenom, another Moses come to lead the Tigers out of the wilderness and into the playoffs. The fans ate it up like popcorn.

The players on the team knew better. There wasn't one of them who didn't dislike Eddie for his selfish style of play. Tension on the team was running high. In particular, Buck Malone remained very hostile toward Eddie. The team was a powder keg on skates. And Bobby was hard-pressed to keep the peace.

Two weeks after King arrived, the Tigers were in Saskatoon for an important game with the Stars. A win would move the Tigers past the Stars into fourth place. A loss would put them back into the cellar.

Because the game was so important, the Tigers arrived in Saskatoon a day early. After an afternoon practice, the team had a free evening for themselves. Bobby Drake decided to take advantage of this extra time by having a long, quiet meal in one of the town's better restaurants.

Just as Bobby was finishing his meal, Gordie Stone came running into the restaurant, looking around wildly. When he spotted Bobby, the little goalie rushed over to him.

"Bobby! I've been looking all over for you. Topay wants to see you right away. At the hotel. It's urgent."

"What's wrong, Gordie? What happened?"

"I'm not sure. Something's happened in the big club." Gordie sat down and caught his breath. "He didn't tell me the details, but it feels like trouble."

Bobby got up. "You got a cab outside, Gordie?"

"Yeah, I told him to wait," he said.

"You coming, Gordie?" Bobby asked.

"No, I'll see you later," he said. "As long as I'm here, I might as well have a bite to eat."

When Bobby arrived at the hotel, Topay was waiting for him in the lobby. He looked worried. Eddie King was with him.

"I just got a call from Clyde Borden" Topay said. "It's about your old teammate, Jack Casey."

Bobby felt his throat tighten. "What about Jack? What's happened?"

"He busted his leg, Bobby," Topay said. "He's going to be out for the rest of the season."

Bobby was stunned. Casey had always seemed like Superman. It was hard to imagine him getting badly hurt.

"They tell me it was a fluke," Topay went on. "Jack was skating along, and he lost the edge on one of his skates. He just fell into the boards. Nobody was near him or anything. A fluke."

"That's bad news," Eddie said quietly. "How's he doing?"

"Jack? Oh, he's all right," Topay said. "It was a clean break, and the doctors think it will mend nicely. Jack's not too thrilled about missing the play-offs, though."

"I guess not," Bobby said. "And neither is the rest of the team, I'll bet. How are they going to replace him?"

"Clyde didn't say. But he'll be flying in for the game tomorrow. I guess he'll be taking someone back with him."

Eddie and Bobby exchanged looks. "Think he'll be taking the kid here, Coach?" Bobby asked.

"That would be my guess," Topay sighed.

The next day was a game day, and the Tigers were on the ice for their morning skate. All except one of them.

It didn't take Buck Malone long to notice who was missing. He cornered Bobby against the boards to find out why.

"What's going on?" Malone snarled. "Where's Eddie King?"

"Back at the hotel, I guess," Bobby said. "I gave him the morning off."

"You what? Are you out of your mind, Bobby?"

"Maybe I am. Did you hear about Jack Casey?"

Malone nodded. "Tough break for old Jack," he said. "A pretty lucky break for Eddie King, though, huh? I suppose they've called him back up?"

"Not officially," Bobby told him. "But Clyde Borden is flying in for tonight's game. The smart money says he's not going back alone."

"It's not fair, Bobby. The kid never did pay his dues."

Bobby shrugged. "Maybe it's better this way."

"Better? He didn't learn a blinking thing down here! And now he's heading back up as happy as you please. I should have nailed him when I had the chance."

"You never *had* the chance, Malone. I was always there to stop you."

Malone snickered. "I'll bet you regret it now, huh?"

"No, I don't regret it," Bobby snapped. "When are you going to grow up, Malone? You can't settle everything with your fists, either on the ice or off it."

"That's my business, Bobby. Tell me something. Did you give him the day off to keep him away from me?"

Bobby faced him squarely. "That's right, Malone. I did."

Malone laughed bitterly. "What's the kid going to do when he doesn't have you around to protect him?"

"What are you going to do, Malone?"

Malone's eyes narrowed. "What do you mean by that?"

"I'm through protecting you. Topay thinks you're poison to the team. And I'm beginning to think he's right."

"I don't believe it, Bobby. You're going to throw me to the wolves after all these years?"

"Put it this way. You foul up once more, and you're finished as a Tiger. I mean it, Malone. Finished."

"You wouldn't."

"Just try me and see," Bobby said flatly.

CHAPTER

5

The big game was the first meeting between the Stars and the new improved Tigers with Eddie King. Fourth place was on the line, and a noisy crowd had packed the Saskatoon arena. The crowd booed loudly as Bobby led the Tigers out onto the ice.

"Sounds like they're up for it," Gordie Stone remarked. "I hope the players are calmer than their fans!"

"Fat chance," Bobby said. His voice was grim. "We're going to have to work tonight, boys. All of us."

The Stars came out and skated around, and the fans screamed wildly. The Tigers had to huddle together to be heard.

"Hey!" someone said. "Look at Number Four. He thinks he's playing football!"

Bobby looked up. The thin kid with the mustache had a football face mask rigged to the bottom of his helmet. He seemed to be skating gingerly.

"Looks like he's playing hurt," Bobby said.

"Him? Don't trust him," Malone warned. "The guy thinks like a snake or something. He's probably faking an injury so he can suck us in!"

The players laughed, and some of the pregame nervousness was broken. They were ready to play. While the team warmed up, Bobby was thinking about Number Four, wondering if he really was hurt.

It didn't take long to find out.

Early in the game, Number Four was chasing a loose puck back into his own zone. Bobby was hot on his heels, looking to take him out and create a scoring opportunity.

Number Four got to the puck first, and tapped it to the side. Bobby went right at him.

The player looked up, saw Bobby coming, and froze. Then he shied away to the left. Bobby only got a piece of him, but it was enough to make the kid wince in pain.

The play went back the other way and was whistled down for a penalty. "Thanks, pops," the kid said through clenched teeth. "I really needed that."

Bobby looked into his face, past the face mask and the droopy mustache. "Wait a minute. You're all wired up!"

Number Four nodded. "I blocked a shot with my face," he said, and laughed bitterly between his teeth. "Guess I was never much in the brains department." He skated away.

On the bench, Bobby passed the word to his teammates.

"I tell you, he's faking it," Malone rasped.

"His jaw's wired shut, Malone," Bobby said. "He wouldn't fake a thing like that!"

"Don't be too sure," Malone said. "I've got a feeling he's out to get one of us tonight." He swung his legs over the boards and skated away.

"Don't be a jerk!" Bobby yelled after him. "He's hurt!"

Eddie King slid over beside Bobby on the bench. "I told you he was crazy," Eddie said.

Bobby reached up to his throat. "You know this claw I wear, Eddie?"

Eddie nodded. "Casey's claw? What about it?"

"I didn't mention it before," Bobby said. "But the darn thing can get pretty heavy sometimes. Know what I mean?"

Out on the ice, the action was heating up. There was a fight for the puck in the corner, close to the Stars' goal. Number Four had possession, but Malone bounced him off the puck and got control. Another of the Stars was in good position. But he went fishing for the puck with his stick, instead of playing the man. Malone got past him.

Number Four tried to get back into the play, but he was too far away. He reached out desperately and took a swipe at the puck. But his aim was high. His blade caught the shaft of Malone's stick and rode up along it.

Bobby watched in horror from the bench as the stick rode all the way up and smashed Malone in the face.

Malone yelped, and dropped his stick and gloves. He put his hands up, grabbing at his nose, and came away with a handful of blood. Then he looked up with murder in his eyes.

"You lousy little faker!" he snarled. "I'll kill you!"

Number Four was backing away slowly. "It was an accident, man," the kid whined through his clenched teeth.

"Faker!" Malone screamed. He moved toward the kid like a fighter stalking his opponent in the ring.

Bobby was off the bench and skating hard. So was Eddie King. But they were too far away.

"Malone!" Bobby yelled. "Stop!" Around the arena, the fans howled in anger.

Malone was beyond listening. He grabbed Number Four by the throat with one huge hand, and ripped off his helmet with the other.

"Malone!" Bobby screamed. It was too late. He'd never get there in time.

Something streaked past Bobby in a blur. He looked up and saw that it was Eddie King, skating for all he was worth straight for Malone. Malone was looking at Number Four and was starting to throw his punch.

Eddie hit Malone with a flying tackle that sent them both smashing into the boards.

Number Four didn't even stop to pick up his helmet. He headed straight for the Stars' bench.

Bobby skated over as Eddie and Malone struggled to their feet. The referee, Henry, was hovering nearby.

"You punk!" Malone gasped. "Who do you think you are?"

Henry spoke up. "I'm calling that a deliberate attempt to injure, Malone. You're out of the game."

"*What?* I didn't even hit him!"

"I don't care, Malone," Henry said. "If this guy hadn't stopped you, you would have clobbered him. Now, get off the ice."

Malone turned to Eddie King. "You made this happen, punk," he said. "It's all your fault." He stepped toward him.

Bobby jumped between them. "I've had it with you, Malone. Get to the dressing room."

"Get out of my way, Bobby," Malone said. "I don't want to have to hit you."

Bobby stood his ground. "Off the ice, Malone. Now!"

"I'm not your dog anymore, Bobby," Malone growled. "Get out of my way!" he slammed his forearm up into Bobby's face, knocking him to the ice. Then he went after Eddie King.

Eddie was ready for him. He caught Malone's wrist and turned with it, twisting it against his other arm in a kind of wrestling hold. Then Eddie put on the pressure, and Malone groaned in pain and crumbled to his knees.

"Try anything and I break the arm," Eddie said softly. Malone squirmed but stayed on his knees.

Bobby struggled to his feet and found he was a bit shaky on his skates. "You OK, Bobby?" Eddie asked.

Bobby looked up. Eddie had Malone on his feet now, still in the armlock. Malone refused to meet Bobby's eyes. There seemed to be little fight left in him now.

"I'm fine," Bobby said. "Thanks for your help, kid."

Together, they took Malone to the runway that led down to the Tigers' dressing room.

"You're through, Malone," Bobby said. "Topay can do what he likes with you. You've just played your last game as a Tiger."

Malone stomped down the runway and slammed the door behind him. Bobby skated wearily back to the bench and sat down.

"It had to be done," Eddie told him softly.

Bobby didn't reply. He had taken out the tiger's claw and was studying it closely. He held the claw lightly in the palm of his hand. "You know something, Eddie? Sometimes I get awfully sick of this captain's job. This team is choking me."

Bobby turned his hand over, and Jack Casey's claw fell to the floor. Bobby kicked it under the bench and smiled. It felt as if a burden had been lifted from his shoulders.

"Hey," Eddie cried, diving under the bench. He came up with the claw in his hand, and he held it out to Bobby. "What are you doing? Take it!"

Bobby shook his head. "No, Eddie. I don't want it anymore. You keep it if you want it."

"Me? What would I do with it?"

"I don't care," Bobby said. "I'm through with this team, kid, just like Malone. I'm going to hand in my notice."

"You're what? What are you going to do? Hockey's your whole life."

Bobby shrugged. "I don't know. Drive a truck? Sell insurance? Something will come up."

Eddie shook his head. "Something's come up right now, man," he said. "It's our turn for a shift on the ice. Come on, snap out of it. For now, you're still a Tiger."

On the ice, Bobby was in a daze. He was skating in molasses and thinking in a fog. One of the Stars came in on Bobby's side and passed the puck into the center. Bobby glanced inside to follow the play, and the winger slipped past him to complete the give-and-go. Only a good save by Gordie Stone stopped it from being a goal.

"Hey, man," Eddie King yelled. "Finish the check!"

Bobby looked at him blankly.

"Come on, Bobby, wake up! We've got to take away their give-and-go. Like this!"

The same winger was coming in on Eddie's side of the ice. He fed in the centering pass, then tried to make the same move he made on Bobby. Eddie crunched him into the boards.

"See?" Eddie called over. "Easy!"

Bobby looked up. Another player was coming in on him with the puck. Bobby forced himself to ignore the puck while he lined the guy up. He played the man all the way and took him to the ice.

The hit made Bobby feel better. It seemed to bring him out of his daze.

"That's the way," Eddie called over. He had a big grin on his face.

Bobby grinned back. "Let's go get 'em, kid!" he yelled.

The Tigers went on to win easily. Eddie King didn't score any goals that night. He and Bobby were too busy dishing out hits on the blue line. But, as usually happens when a team plays sound defensive hockey, enough Tigers found the net to give them a 4-2 victory.

The team came off the ice yelling and screaming, slapping each other on the back. They were happy, and they had a right to be. The Tigers were headed for the play-offs.

6

Bobby found Bill Topay and Clyde Borden together in the little room provided for the visiting coach. Topay jumped up when he saw him coming.

"Come in, Bobby," he said. Great game!"

"Yeah," Bobby muttered. "Is Malone still around?"

"No," Topay said. "He came flying though here as if he were late for a meeting with the governor. Did you talk to him, Bobby?"

"Yeah. I told him he was through. Finished."

"Did you, now?" Clyde Borden's eyebrows went up. "That's the best news I've had all week!"

Bobby glared at him. "I'm glad we made your day, Clyde."

"Oh, don't get me wrong," Borden said. "I like Malone. But I've been waiting for him to quit for a long time. I want to hire him as a scout."

That stopped Bobby cold. "A scout?"

"Of course!" Borden said with an embarrassed laugh. "I'm an assistant general manager in the NHL, Bobby. Do you think I *enjoy* flying around the country like a messenger boy?"

"But, Malone—"

"Oh, I know he's a real hardhead and a fighter," Borden said. "But he's been loyal to the organization. We have to take care of him. You know, he's only become bitter the past few seasons as his playing skills began to go. Now, he'll be able to stay in the game without the pressure of having to play. He'll love being a scout."

Bobby thought of Malone flying around the country and spending time with all the players and coaches. Borden was right. He'd love it.

"My other problem is this, Bobby. I need a defenseman for the big club, and pronto!"

"I don't know if I can help you there," Bobby said. "The Tigers will be short two men now."

"Two men short? Who's the other one?"

"I am," Bobby said. "I'm quitting."

"What?" Borden gasped.

"Bobby," Topay began, "you can't—"

"I've made up my mind," Bobby said. "If you really want me to, I'll play out the season. But in the spring I'll be leaving the team for good."

"The spring?" Borden said. "I was hoping you'd want to leave sooner than that."

"What for, Clyde? You need another scout?"

"No. I want you to play defense, Bobby. In the NHL."

"Me?" Bobby was shocked. "But what about the kid?"

"Eddie doesn't have the experience," Borden said. "We need a guy who can steady the defense and settle things down. A leader, Bobby. Someone who can fill Jack Casey's skates."

Bobby looked at Topay. "But the Tigers need me," he said lamely.

Topay looked him in the eye. "It's your decision, Bobby. Five minutes ago you were ready to leave us high and dry. I guess we'll get by, whatever you decide."

"Well, Bobby," Borden asked, "how about it?"

"I need some time," Bobby said. "This is too sudden. I've got to think."

Borden looked at his watch. "Think all you want," he said. "My plane leaves in two hours."

When Bobby went out into the hallway, Eddie King was waiting for him.

"Well?" Eddie said. "Did you quit?"

"They want me to go *up!*" Bobby said. "To the NHL!"

Eddie's face broke into a grin. "That's great, man!" he said. "Congratulations!"

"I don't think I'll be going," Bobby said. "If I play at all, I think I should play for the Tigers."

"That's nonsense. You play where you deserve to play."

Bobby looked at him. "What about the Tigers? What happens to them?"

"Don't worry about the Tigers. We can take care of ourselves." Eddie opened his collar. Hanging at his throat was Jack Casey's claw.

"*You?*"

"You gave it up. So I though I'd take it on. We may be losing our captain, but we've still got our King!"

Bobby shook his head and laughed. "I thought all you cared about was your stats! What's with the change of heart?"

Eddie shrugged. "I don't know," he said with a shy smile. "I just figured I'd better learn something about responsibility and leadership while I'm down here. I'll need those kinds of skills if I'm ever going to be as good as a Jack Casey. Or a Bobby Drake."

"Thanks, kid," Bobby said. They shook hands. "Good luck. I'm sure you'll make a fine captain. And I'm sure you'll be back up in the bigs before long."

Bobby started running back down the hallway. He felt like a ten-year-old kid again, starting out on a brand new adventure.

It was a very good feeling.

Willie's Choice

William Warren

1

The kid's hard jab landed squarely on Willie's chin. It snapped his head back before his eyes could warn his brain that the punch was coming. He felt the force of the blow all the way down to his toes.

Before Willie could react, he received two more hard shots. One was below the beltline, although the ref didn't seem to notice. The other was a blow to the side of his head that made his ears ring. Willie lunged forward, arms reaching, trying to hook the kid's arms and tie him up.

The kid danced away easily. He covered his escape with a pair of stinging jabs and paused near the center of the ring. There he eyed Willie coldly as he bounced up and down on his toes. He seemed to be enjoying himself.

Willie followed him, not with any real hope of catching him, but because that was his style. It was the only style he knew.

Willie Benson was a hard-nosed boxer, a banger. He was willing to take ten punches in order to give one of his own. That style had worked for Rocky Marciano—and it had worked for Willie Benson, too, once upon a time. But that was long ago.

Twenty years of punches had left their marks on Willie's face and body. As a result, his fighting style often worked more in his opponents' favor than his own. It made him a target, as surely as if he had painted large bull's-eyes on his chest and chin.

The kid stopped dancing and stood his ground, waiting for Willie. His arms lay flat against his sides.

Willie pushed out a left jab. The kid dodged it with ease. Willie doubled up on it, hoping to catch the kid by surprise, but again he slipped the punch. Willie threw a hard right. The kid merely leaned away from it like Muhammad Ali did in his prime.

The kid still had not taken a step, and he had not thrown another punch. He seemed to know that he could hit Willie whenever he wanted to. For now, though, he was content to impress the cheering crowd with his blazing speed and defense.

Willie, for his part, noticed none of this. His mind noted only that the kid wasn't moving and therefore was asking to be hit. So Willie kept on giving the kid his best shots, none of which landed. It was only midway through the second round of a ten round fight, but already Willie's mouth was open and he was breathing heavily. The kid, on the other hand, had hardly worked up a sweat.

Willie waded forward and managed to land a hard right to the stomach before the kid tied him up. Then, with his right glove hooked behind Willie's left elbow, the kid slid his other hand around Willie's neck. He began tugging downward in classic Ali style. Willie guessed that someone—the kid, his manager, or both— had studied Ali's old fight films.

It was a neat move. Willie tried to bang away at the kid's ribs and side with his free hand. But the downward pressure on his head and neck was too great. By the time the referee finally stepped in to separate them, Willie's upper body was bent forward as if he were bowing before a king.

The kid moved away and began circling to his left. Willie went after him but could not close the distance between them. Willie hoped to get the kid on the ropes or trap him in a corner. If he did, he could work the kid's midsection with hammering blows from both fists. *That* would take some of the bounce out of those strong young legs!

The kid wasn't about to let that happen, though—not yet, anyway. He was following his manager's shouted advice to "Stick and move! Stick and move!" He dipped and darted here and there, staying out of Willie's range. Every now and then he stopped to fire sharp, crisp jabs to Willie's face. The blows made Willie feel as if he had run head first into a wall.

After each jab the kid was on his bicycle again, moving away from Willie with the grace and ease of a deer.

Then, with ten seconds remaining in the round, the kid stopped running. He slid forward and delivered six punches with machine-gun quickness.

Startled, Willie tried to cover up. But all that did was hide the last punch, a hard right cross, from Willie's view. It landed solidly on the side of Willie's jaw. He was not even aware that he had been hit. Suddenly, though, his legs would not hold him up and something was pulling his face down to the canvas.

As Willie lay facedown on the mat, he knew he should be getting up. But for the life of him, he couldn't remember why.

He thought he heard a bell go off. But he couldn't tell if it was the bell signaling the end of the round, or if it was just a ringing in his head. The sound seemed far away, and he had to strain to hear it. It was like listening to a distant foghorn and trying to figure out where the boat was in the water.

Willie shook his head to clear it. Staring down at him was the concerned face of his manager, Al Gardner. Willie got to his feet slowly. Al and Willie's trainer, Joe Dundy, helped Willie over to his corner. As Willie walked with them, he looked out at the ringside crowd. When he saw that most of the people were still in their seats, he realized the fight wasn't over yet.

"Come on, champ, we got to get to work on you," Al said. He and Joe Dundy pushed Willie down onto the corner stool. Willie thought that sounded like a very good idea—but he didn't know why. His mind drifted in and out of focus like a distant radio station. "Thanks," he mumbled, "but I think I've had enough to drink."

The ammonia capsule waved before his nose by Joe Dundy brought Willie back to his senses. He twisted his head away and pushed aside Dundy's hand. He knew where he was now, and what had happened to him. He had gone down, but the bell had saved him.

The ring doctor came over and used a penlight to look deeply into Willie's eyes. He asked Willie a couple of questions about who and where he was. Then, nodding that Willie was all right, he left. Joe Dundy went to work on Willie next. At the same time Al Gardner began talking quickly in his high-pitched voice.

"You're not cutting the ring off on him, Willie," he said. "You're letting him get away from you. You've got to cut the ring off and get him against the ropes. Then bang away at him till he can't take any more."

Willie nodded. He knew Al was right, because Al was his manager and managers were always right. Al could see things going on in the ring that Willie couldn't see because he was right in the middle of the action. It was Al's job to be right. And it was Willie's job to do as he was told. Willie accepted those facts as gospel truth. Al kept talking, and Willie glanced across the ring at his opponent.

The kid, whose name was Randy "Lightning" Liggett, was standing in his corner with his arms draped across the ring ropes. He was tall and lean for a heavyweight. And he was a young and hungry fighter. The huge paychecks that would someday make him wealthy, fat, and lazy were still ahead of him. He had won all eight of his previous bouts, all by knockouts. But he was still learning, still trying to make a name for himself. His manager was bringing him along slowly. That meant that he was boosting the kid's record at the expense of over-the-hill fighters like Willie Benson.

The kid looked at Willie sitting heavily on his stool and smiled. It was the kind of smile that spiders give to passing flies.

And it was the smile, more than anything else, that got to Willie. It made him want to turn things around in his favor, at least for a while. He vowed to show the kid that the old man still had a few tricks left.

"The kid's a stiff, Willie," Al said. "I've been in boxing 48 years. I've seen more stiffs than a funeral director. He's a stiff."

The warning horn sounded. Willie opened his mouth to receive his mouthpiece. He clenched his teeth around it and rose from the stool. Suddenly he felt a thousand years old. "One of us is a stiff, Al," he thought, "but it's not the kid. The kid's not the one who's being paid to take a dive in five."

Then the bell rang for Round Three. Willie took a deep breath and marched forward to meet the kid in the center of the ring.

2

The kid met Willie with another of those stinging left jabs that had given him the name "Lightning." Willie brushed at his nose with his glove. He sent out a jab of his own. It was short by at least eight inches.

Liggett was flat-footed now, so Willie moved forward in a hurry. To his surprise Liggett didn't back up or dance away this time. Instead he chose to slug it out with Willie in the center of the ring. Or maybe he just wanted to show Willie that he could take punches as well as dish them out.

Willie thought it was a silly thing for the kid to try to prove. All Liggett had to do to win the fight was keep moving. He only needed his jab to keep Willie away from him. Still, he was acting the way a lot of kids did who were learning the ropes in boxing.

Because a lot of young fighters didn't have a style of their own, they tried to copy everything they had seen. Whatever Ali or Sugar Ray Leonard or Larry Holmes had done in the ring, they tried to do in every fight. You could count on it, as sure as sunrise. And sometimes, if you waited long enough, you could use their mistakes to beat them.

One minute you'd find them standing still, bobbing and weaving with their guards down like Sugar Ray. The next minute they'd be doing the Ali shuffle to dazzle the crowd with their fancy footwork. Then you'd find them on the ropes, urging you forward to play "rope-a-dope." And sometimes they decided to show you—and the crowd too, of course—that they were sluggers as well as dancers and dodgers.

That was when you could get them. And maybe leave a few calling cards of your own.

It didn't always work that way, of course. Willie's flat nose and an enlarged ear proved that. But when it happened, Willie had a fighting chance—at least until they decided to switch styles again.

So Willie waded in, working on the kid's midsection. He had always been a good body puncher. The stomach, Willie knew, was easier to hit than the head. A head could bob and weave, but the stomach was always right there in front of you. Besides, there was always the possibility that he could do some rib damage. That would give the guy something to think about before his next fight.

The trouble tonight was that the kid was winning the war on the inside, too. He was always in motion, blocking Willie's punches with his gloves or his arms. Or else he was sending hard body shots of his own that surprised Willie with their power. Most young boxers were headhunters—again, in the manner of Ali, who seldom threw many body punches. But this kid seemed to understand that it is better (and less painful) to give than to receive, whether by headhunting or body punching.

Still, while the early part of the third round was mostly even, Willie managed to land his best blows of the fight. One was a solid left hook to the kid's ribs. He followed it quickly with a wild right hand that caught Liggett on the side of the head.

The kid backed away, eyes wide. He was shocked to find out that the old man still could pack such a punch.

But then Liggett let his head wobble from side to side, and his knees moved in and out weakly. He laughed and danced away, showing Willie that he really wasn't hurt after all. The crowd screamed and howled its approval. The kid was giving them the show they had come to see.

"Give it up, old man," Liggett taunted as he danced around Willie. He shot out a jab that caught Willie in the mouth. It split his lip. Willie swallowed the blood and kept after the kid as he moved around the ring.

In his earlier years, the taste of blood had angered Willie. But if he had learned one thing in his 20 years in the ring, it was the art of self-control. It didn't pay to lose your head in the ring. Your opponent might use dirty tactics such as low blows, or thumbing you in the eye, or raking your face with the laces of his gloves. But if you lost your head, you usually lost the fight as well. It never paid to stop thinking in the ring.

Besides, it wasn't as if Willie had never been cut before. His nose had been broken twice. Now it was mashed almost flat against his face. His brows were thick with scars from old cuts around his eyes. And once, while he was a club fighter, an opponent had fought him with thumbtacks hidden in the padding of his gloves. After the fight, Willie's manager had looked at his torn, bleeding face and remarked sadly, "Guess you'll never be a fashion model now, kid."

While the bleeding from his lip didn't bother Willie, it had a strange effect on the kid. Liggett's eyes opened wide, and then they sort of glazed over. He bared his teeth in a savage grin and almost ran at Willie in his hurry to get to him. When he got close, Liggett let loose with a storm of lightning blows.

They were deadly punches—hard jabs, uppercuts, and wild swinging right hands that could have knocked down a horse. They came from all angles, one after the other, without stopping. All Willie could do was try to cover up until the kid got tired and stopped his attack.

Willie backed up slowly until he was against the ropes. He could hear the kid grunting, "Huh!-Huh!-Huh!" with every punch he threw. Willie's constant bobbing and weaving caused many of the kid's punches to miss. But those that landed felt like hammers. Willie wanted to fight back, but the kid wasn't giving him a chance.

Then suddenly the kid stopped punching. He reached out with his left glove and held it against Willie's face.

It wasn't a punch. He was doing what fight people call "measuring the opponent."

They said that it told a fighter how far he was from his opponent. But in fact it did nothing of the sort. Fighters almost always knew when they were within punching range. What the move actually did was to block Willie's view.

And then, before Willie knew what was coming, he took a blow to the head from the kid's right hand. It almost buckled his knees. It was a glancing blow, but Willie's eyes crossed and uncrossed from the impact.

"Well," he thought, "two can play that game. If he wants to measure me, I'll give

him something to measure!" He knew that
the kid would try it again, because it had
worked so well the last time.

Willie waited until Liggett repeated the
same "measuring" movements. He counted
silently to himself, "one, two," knowing that
the kid would be firing another hard right.
But if Willie's timing was good . . .

Suddenly Willie bobbed backward and
leaned to his right. Then he lunged forward
and threw a hard right just as the kid's
own right hand was starting on its way.
Willie beat him to the punch.

He caught the kid flush on the jaw, and
down he went. Down onto the seat of his
purple trunks. Down onto his back with
his feet high in the air, purple shoelace
tassels flying. The kid's mouth was wide
open, and he had a vacant look in his
eyes.

Liggett was sitting up now, looking
around in a daze. You'd almost have sworn
that he was thinking, "Did anybody get
the license number of that truck?"

"Five . . . Six . . ."

The kid was on one knee now. He was
shaking his head, trying to regain his
senses.

Meanwhile, Willie was dancing in his corner. He was charged up with the feeling of victory in the air. The crowd was on its feet, shouting. A few people were cheering for the upset in the making. Far more were pleading for their hero, a local boy, to come back and teach the old man a lesson.

And then it hit Willie, harder than the hardest blow he had taken from the kid. He was supposed to *lose* the fight, not win by a knockout.

Certain parties had warned him that some big money was riding on his taking a dive in the fifth round. His help, they had said, would earn him $5,000. Willie had nodded and said, "Yeah. OK," to them. There was nothing else he could say. Unless, that is, he'd rather take a dive in 40 feet of water wearing cement boots.

3

Willie frowned at the thought of what he had done. Then he thought of what could happen to him if the kid failed to beat the referee's count.

"Get up, you bum!" he called out. Then, aware of how his words might sound, he added quickly, "So I can beat up on you some more!"

Liggett managed to beat the count, but just barely. He was shaky on his feet. His eyes were as glassy as a stuffed moose's. The ref wiped his gloves clean and asked him if he was all right. Then he stepped back to let the fight go on.

Willie figured that if the kid made it to his feet, the ref wouldn't stop the fight. After all, the kid was a hometown hero.

He had the crowd in his corner. It was also possible, though unlikely, that the same people who had talked to Willie had talked to the ref as well. In any event, the cards seemed stacked in Liggett's favor. No one wanted or expected a has-been like Willie Benson to beat an up-and-comer like this kid.

Liggett was still dazed. Looking into his glassy eyes, Willie thought that he could see all the way inside his head. Still, the kid had enough wits about him to keep moving. He was trying to stay away from Willie until his head cleared. It wasn't hard to do, either. Willie at his best had never been a light-footed boxer. He was getting very tired. His legs were starting to feel as if he were wearing ten-pound ankle weights.

The bell rang. Round Three was over. Willie returned to his corner and sat down. Sweat poured off him. Joe Dundy began to mop at him with a wet sponge.

"You were great, Willie," Al Gardner said with a grin. "You did just like I told you."

"No, I didn't, Al," Willie argued.

Al paused and stared at him. Willie almost never spoke between rounds unless someone asked him a question. But this time he wanted Al to know that his strategy hadn't worked. Al had told him to cut off the ring and trap the kid on the ropes.

"I didn't get him on the ropes," Willie went on. "He got *me* on the ropes. I hit him while he had me on the ropes."

"Yeah, well, it worked out the same, didn't it?" Al replied. "Now, here's what you've got to do this round Willie. . . . "

Willie looked across the ring. This time, the kid was sitting down. His trainer was waving an ammonia capsule in front of his nose. The kid didn't seem to want any of it. Willie knew the feeling.

As Al and Joe worked on him, Willie thought about the strategy for the next round. He knew that because he had knocked Liggett down, things had suddenly changed. The referee had almost surely scored the last round in Willie's favor. So, at the most, the kid led 2-1 in rounds.

Willie figured he could even up the fight in the next round. He wouldn't even need another knockdown. All he had to do was to get in some solid body punches—and avoid getting knocked down himself.

Then the words entered his mind once again, like an old song you hear over and over on the radio. *Take a dive in five, Willie, if you know what's good for you.* And suddenly Willie thought, "Why the heck am I worrying about evening up this fight? It's not going past the fifth round anyway."

The bell rang for Round Four. Willie rose and came forward. He expected the kid to be on his toes, dancing and throwing long-range punches. Instead the kid came in at a walk, grim faced. He delivered a left that was so low it hit Willie in the midthigh. The referee said nothing.

Willie threw a jab that glanced off the kid's ear. He followed it with a right to the ribs. He was tiring rapidly now, and he knew that his punches were losing their steam. He felt as if he were carrying a piano on his back. A hard right to his forehead snapped his head back, and the kid sent another punch south of the border. Willie stepped back and frowned at the ref. He shook his head to indicate that it wasn't a low blow.

A voice inside of Willie's head screamed, "What does he have to do, ref? Hit me in the socks?" But he said nothing. If you make the ref mad, he could always find a way to take a round, or even the fight, away from you.

Suddenly the kid backed up and danced away.

That was the way it went when you were young, Willie thought. Even when you'd been hurt, it didn't take long to get your strength back. But as you got older, it seemed that every hard punch took a little more out of your legs. Finally, you had nothing left in them. And as Willie knew from his long, painful past, you couldn't go the distance when you were out of gas and riding on two flat tires.

Liggett switched his attack to Willie's head. The kid was back to his stick-and-move tactics now. He was sending out hard jabs that landed on Willie's face more often than they missed.

Willie plodded ahead, trying not to show the pain he felt whenever another of the kid's punches landed. His face was beginning to swell around his eyes. But still he came on, trying to cut off the ring and corner the kid.

A left hook from Liggett opened a small cut at the corner of Willie's eyebrow. Willie began to press his attack, throwing wild, wide punches whenever the kid came within range. He knew that he was wrong to lose his self-control. But he also knew that the ref might use the cut as an excuse to stop the fight.

It was only a small cut now, a thin trickle of blood. But if the cut grew worse and he couldn't see when the blood got in his eye, the ref might not have to stop the fight. The kid was still strong enough to end the fight himself.

Liggett was more careful this time, though. He didn't come after Willie like an attacking shark at the sight of Willie's blood. Instead, he stalked Willie as a big-game hunter stalks a wounded tiger in the jungle.

Willie dabbed at his eye with a glove. He smiled to himself. The kid had learned his lesson. But that didn't make Willie's task any easier. Liggett kept flicking out long jabs that found the cut as if they were guided by radar. Willie tried to block the punches, but his reflexes were slower than ever. And he couldn't block the punches that he didn't see coming.

The cut was getting worse, and Willie's eyes were tiny slits now from the pounding his face had taken. He had to admit that

Liggett was controlling the fight.

Then, midway through the round, Willie noticed that something strange was happening. The kid seemed to be slowing down. He wasn't throwing punches in flurries anymore. And his punches weren't landing with the same power as before. He still danced every now and then, but not for as long or with as much pep as he had earlier. He seemed willing to let Willie tie him up in the center of the ring. And when they clinched, it was the kid who was doing the most holding on.

Willie almost laughed out loud as it dawned on him that the kid had punched himself out. Tired as he was himself, Willie wanted to say, "Hey, kid haven't you ever been tired before? Wait till you're 40. Then you'll know what tired really is!"

He said nothing, though. Instead, he tried to fight his way out of another clinch. His arms felt like barbells. Still, just knowing that the kid was nearly as tired as he was gave him a mental boost. It made him feel stronger and younger somehow.

Willie knew it was the kid's first ten-round bout. Even worse for him, it was the first time he had ever gone more than three rounds in his pro career. His first eight fights had all been early-round knockouts. The fact was that he simply wasn't ready to go ten hard rounds with anybody.

There was no way Liggett could have prepared himself for what was happening to him. It was a problem that most young boxers had, especially if they were heavyweights. It was something you only learned by going the distance. And how could you learn to pace yourself for ten rounds when you knocked out every opponent in the early rounds? And how could you help but knock out the bums your manager kept feeding you to make your record look good?

Willie saw the kid's problem. He had been there himself, so many years ago that he could hardly remember.

4

At 19 Willie had been an up-and-coming young boxer. The papers had all said that he would be the next heavyweight champ. He was fighting then under the name Willie "The Hammer" Benson. He was 14-0, with a dozen knockouts to his credit as a six-round boxer.

In his first ten-rounder, he had gone up against a huge aging fighter named Joe "Sudden Death" Johnson. At the weigh-in, the 6-foot-5-inch, 225-pound man had glared down at him and growled, "What are you doin' with a name like Willie? You ain't Willie Mays!"

Willie had laughed. And then he said, "Yeah, well, you ain't Lyndon Johnson, either."

The first round of the fight showed Willie Benson's style. He took some hard punches in order to deliver his own. And the older man was perfectly willing to trade punches with Willie. Both fighters exchanged several jabs, and then Johnson moved inside to tie up Willie's arms. It was then that Willie learned his first great lesson in boxing.

As they came together, "Sudden Death" banged three heavy punches in Willie's stomach. Then, holding on, he grunted "Gonna *destroy* you tonight, boy. And when it's over, I'm gonna go after your momma and daddy and destroy them, too!"

Willie lost all his control. He had never been so angry in his entire life. For the next two rounds he chased the older man and put everything he had into every punch he threw. He swung wildly from the hip, throwing long, looping punches with both hands, trying to punish Johnson for his threats. Some of the punches got through and landed. Most of them either missed or were blocked by Johnson's gloves.

Then suddenly, about midway through the third round, Willie reached his moment of truth. His strength left him in a rush, like water shooting out of a hole in a barrel. He felt as if he had been fighting for hours—not for less than twelve minutes.

Now Joe "Sudden Death" Johnson moved in to take him apart.

Whump! "Gonna punish you, boy!"

Whump! "Gonna mess up your *face!*"

Whump! "Gonna make you wish you'd never seen the likes of *me!*"

Willie went down twice—once in the third round and once in the fourth. The second time he stayed down for the count.

After the fight Johnson visited Willie's corner, where Willie was sitting on his stool. The big man bent over, draped his arm across Willie's shoulders, and spoke softly. "Sorry about that, kid. I only did what I had to do. Don't let it get you down. You're going to be a real good boxer one of these days. You mark my words."

Willie did become a good boxer after that. But he never did reach the heights that people had expected him to. Instead he became what is known in boxing as a "hanger-on." He was good enough to win most of his fights, but not quite good enough to earn a title shot. He was good enough to give the best heavyweights a real test, but not quite good enough to beat them.

Gradually, Willie (and everybody else) lost track of his age and of his won-lost record as well. Years passed. Vietnam came and went. The world changed—but not Willie Benson. Like Archie Moore, his goal was to fight forever. It was all he knew how to do. It was all he wanted to do.

He had never married or developed any interests outside the ring. Boxing demanded too much. Boxing was his life. It had been so ever since he put on gloves for the first time as a skinny 17-year-old. Even now, more than 20 years later, the best times in his life were when he was training for his next bout. Only then and during the fights did he really feel alive. He could not have told himself or anyone else why this was so. He only knew that boxing fulfilled him in ways that nothing else had. He dreaded the day when he would have to give it up.

And now, with Liggett hanging on for dear life like a tired dancing partner, Willie knew that the fight was his to win or lose.

The kid was huffing and puffing like the Big Bad Wolf. But his punches were more like the Three Little Pigs. Willie was tired, too—but it was different with him. He had no legs left, but then he hadn't started out with good legs anyway. He could go ten rounds on those legs. At least he could if he forgot there were people expecting him to lie down in the next round. He was surprised how often he *did* keep forgetting that fact. Well, 20 years of trying your best to win will make you think that way.

He knew he could win if he could keep Liggett busy and not let him rest. And for a banger like Willie Benson, that wasn't hard to do. It was the same fight plan he had used since before the kid was born.

Willie decided to work on the kid's mind. Give him a few things to think about.

"Getting tired, kid?" He sent a hard right to Liggett's ribs. "Only six more rounds to go."

"Same as you, old man," Liggett grunted. He reached behind Willie's head, tugging it downward.

Willie threw two more rights to the kid's midsection. Then he stepped away from Liggett, stood up, and moved inside again. He pounded away at the kid's stomach.

The bell rang, ending the fourth round.

Willie looked his opponent in the eye. "I'll be waiting for you, kid," he said. He turned and walked to his corner before Liggett could reply.

"Great round, Willie!" Al Gardner said as the weary fighter sat down heavily on his stool. The trainer went to work on Willie's brow, and Al applied a special metal bar to the puffed flesh around his eyes. The bar was kept on ice between rounds, and when it was pressed firmly against the boxer's face, it helped keep swelling down.

Willie nodded without hearing what Al was saying about Round Five. He was thinking about the dive he was supposed to take the next round.

He hadn't been totally surprised when the gamblers had approached him a few days before. He had always known there were people around who paid to fix fights. After all, you don't stay in the fight game for 20 years without learning about all the players. And he knew that fighters his age, nearing the end of the line, made the best candidates for these gamblers. Most aging fighters put up very little protest and took the money that was offered. There was nothing for them to gain by winning since their careers were almost over anyway.

Now that Willie thought about it, what did surprise him was how he'd managed to stay clear of that side of boxing all these years. Well, he was an honest man, and he'd always surrounded himself with honest handlers. Al and Joe were decent and honest men, and they had been with him for nearly his entire career. Willie knew that was why the gamblers had come directly to him. Put the pressure and the threats right on the guy doing the fighting. That was the smartest way to go.

Willie looked across the ring at Liggett. The kid had a small smile on his face. Willie wondered if the kid knew about the fix. Willie had heard that Liggett had some big money boys behind him. So, it was possible he knew what was going on.

More likely though, no one had told him that Willie was going to throw the fight.

Why not let him think he'd won the fight on his own? It might hurt his confidence if he learned that his own people weren't sure he could beat an old pug like Willie without help.

"It's not fair!" Willie thought. "A guy shouldn't have to lose a fight on purpose, just because some gamblers want him to. Not when the guy had spent his whole life trying his best to be a good boxer. I won't do it. I'll . . . "

The bell rang. Round Five had begun.

CHAPTER

5

Liggett began the fifth round on his toes, dancing. But soon his legs reminded him of how tired he was, and he settled down to a slower step.

There was little bobbing and weaving as the two tired fighters slowly circled each other. They had taken each other's best shots, and each had gone down once. They were more careful now. It would be a war to the finish. Neither fighter wanted to make a costly mistake that would lose the war.

Above their heads the lights shone brightly on the ring. Beyond, the crowd was like a large, dark noisy animal with hundreds of faces. Both fighters could hear voices shouting from the crowd and local

TV and radio announcers describing the action from ringside.

The kid let Willie get inside, and Willie noticed Liggett was throwing shorter punches than before. Willie guessed that his manager had told him to slow down, use shorter punches, and save something for the later rounds. It was good advice. Sometimes young boxers had to be reminded that short punches could do as much damage as longer, looping ones.

As they wrestled against the ropes, Willie decided to finish what he had started the round before. He waited for the right moment, which came after he dug a left hook into the kid's side.

"Gonna bust you up, kid," he grunted. He blocked a hook from the kid and buried two more hooks in Liggett's ribs. "And after the fight, I'm going to look up your girlfriend and bust her up, too. Maybe do a paint job on her." A "paint job" was boxing slang for beating someone up until he was bleeding from several cuts on his face.

The younger man snarled and pushed Willie away roughly. "I'll do a paint job on *you*," he growled. Then he waded into Willie, fists flying.

Willie backed up against the ropes and covered up. He held his elbows in tight against his stomach. He put his gloves against the sides of his head. He bobbed and weaved, not wanting to give the kid a clear target for the bombs he was throwing.

Tired as the kid was, anger had delivered new strength to his punches. Willie could hear voices shouting from Liggett's corner. His manager and trainer were urging him, "Slow down. Take it easy!"

The crowd was on its feet now. People were screaming for their hero to finish off the old man. The kid didn't hear them. In his rage, all he could hear were the voices inside his head. They were telling him to take out the old bum with the wise mouth. He hammered away at Willie, but his punches were too wild, too hasty.

Even so, Willie wondered how long he could go on taking the kid's best shots without going down. He had lost his mouthpiece. Every blow he took felt as if he were being hit with a baseball bat. He knew that an uppercut to the jaw would finish him off. But the kid was swinging so wildly he couldn't find the opening between Willie's gloves.

And then, as quickly as the passing of a summer storm, the action halted.

Willie, bent over and peeking between his gloves, got a good look at "Lightning" Liggett. The kid was standing with his mouth wide open, breathing fast. His arms hung limply at his sides.

If possible, Willie was even worse for the wear than Liggett. The cut on his brow had opened again, and a second cut had opened on his right cheek. His body, arms, and face hurt with a pain that would last for a week.

Still, his plan had worked. He had taken the best that the kid could dish out, and he had survived. Now it was time to see if he still had enough strength left to make his gamble pay off.

He came off the ropes and went after the younger man. Willie felt as if he were moving in slow motion—which, indeed, he was. But the kid made no effort to avoid him. Instead, he waited until Willie threw a punch and then hooked Willie's glove with his arm. After throwing a few light taps at Willie's head, he pulled Willie close. The referee stepped in and moved them apart.

The rest of Round Five followed the same pattern—Willie punching his way in, and the kid tying up his arms or wrestling with him in the clinches. Willie couldn't land the punch that might have turned out the kid's lights. And for his part, the kid seemed content to take a punch or two and then tie up Willie until the referee parted them again.

The bell rang.

Willie retreated to his corner. He felt as worn out and beat up as a ten-year-old pair of shoes. And yet he felt very good, too. If not physically, then mentally. He'd won his own personal fight in his mind— a fight he'd been waging since those gamblers had told him to take a dive.

Deep down Willie had realized this was probably going to be his last fight. It was a truth he hadn't wanted to face. But after five rounds with this kid, it was clear Willie had reached the end of the road. Because it was also clear that Liggett wasn't that good a fighter. Perhaps he wasn't a stiff, as Al had claimed. But he wasn't smart enough or strong enough to make it over the long run as a professional boxer. Sure, he could look pretty good against a guy like Willie. But Willie was almost *twice* the kid's age.

From Willie's standpoint, if he was getting whipped by a kid like Liggett, whose only weapon was speed, then he'd better hang 'em up. And if this was going to be Willie's last fight, he was certain of one thing. He wasn't going out with his face pressed against the canvas just because some two-bit hoodlums had *told* him to lie down. He might lose this fight anyway—but not that way.

As Al and Joe finished working on him, Al said, "Willie, you look pretty bad. You want me to stop it?"

Willie turned quickly to Al and said loudly, "No, no. I can outlast this kid, Al. I want to go the distance. Sure, I'm tired. But so is he. Maybe I can get lucky and catch him with a hard one."

"I don't think you can knock him out, Willie," Al said.

"I want to try," Willie said. "And I don't want you throwing in the towel."

Al patted Willie on the shoulder. "OK, Willie, whatever you say. Go get him."

CHAPTER
6

Despite Al's encouragement, the next three rounds were anything but exciting. The two tired fighters lay against each other most of the time, trading weak punches that bored the crowd. Many of the fans got up and left. Some of the rest were booing. In the eighth round, people began throwing things into the ring.

Try as he might, Willie couldn't finish off his opponent. He'd shot his wad in the fifth round and was now paying the price for it. Every punch he threw felt as if his arms had 50-pound weights on them. The kid had slowed down, so it was a little easier for Willie to hit him. But Willie's punches had very little effect on Liggett. Willie knew he didn't have much chance of knocking out the kid.

As for Liggett, he almost seemed to have lost interest in the fight. After the seventh round, Willie had watched the kid's handlers practically begging him to go after Willie. The kid had sat on his stool and just stared across at Willie without much expression on his face as his trainer rubbed his arms and legs. The same thing happened after the eighth round, only this time the kid's manager looked angry. Liggett seemed to pay more attention to what he was being told. When the bell rang for the ninth round, it showed.

The kid came out with a flurry of punches and went after Willie's head. After a few seconds he had reopened the cut on Willie's brow.

This time the cut wouldn't close up. The ring doctor studied it long and hard.

Finally, he looked at the referee and shook his head. That was it. The fight was over.

"No!" Willie yelled. He spat out his mouthpiece. "Don't do this to me! I can *beat* this guy!"

The referee shook his head sadly as the kid waved his arms in triumph. "Sorry, Willie, I can't help it. It's the rules."

Al took Willie by the arm and led him back to his corner.

"I tried, Al," Willie said with tears in his half-closed eyes. "I tried as hard as I could."

"I know," Al said gently as he started cutting away the laces on Willie's gloves.

Willie spoke to Liggett when the kid dropped by the dressing room afterward. He said to the kid, "Nice fight. I still think I could have taken you before the final bell."

Liggett laughed and shook his head. "No way, old man" he said. "I'm as quick as a flick of your Bic." But then they locked eyes, and Liggett dropped the joking, bragging tone. He lowered his voice and said, "But you ain't bad for an old guy. Not bad at all. You must have been somebody once."

They shook hands. Liggett left. Willie looked around. Al had gone home, and so had everybody else. Willie got up slowly and headed for the door, feeling a million years old.

He froze as he turned down the long hall. There they were—a tall one, a short one, and somebody else between them. He was sure they were waiting for him.

He sighed and shuddered with fatigue. But then he squared his shoulders and walked right toward them. "I made my choice," he said to himself. "I did what I had to do, and I'm not sorry for it."

The light was behind the three men who stood blocking the hallway. Willie stopped. He couldn't see their faces.

"All right," he said, "you might as well give it to me here and now. I may be a washed-up old pug, but I never threw a fight and I never will. I don't care what you do. It's all over for me, anyhow. Tonight was my last fight."

Willie braced himself for whatever might happen next. He was surprised to hear a low chuckle from one of the men.

"Go on, get it over with!" Wilie's words came out in a rush. "I was supposed to run out of steam and I didn't. I just couldn't. I don't know what kind of joke this is, but —"

The chuckle was louder this time. "Take it easy, Willie," a deep voice said. "You've taken enough punishment for one night. We're here to make sure you get home in one piece."

One of the men turned into the light and flashed his badge as identification. "Our unit has been tailing those gamblers for weeks," he explained. "We knew all about the fix. We're here to tell you that the guys who were leaning on you won't be leaning on *anybody* for a long time."

"That was quite a fight," said the third man. "Really something for an old guy. How about letting us drive you home so you can get a good rest?"

Willie sighed deeply. All the tension in his body seemed to drain away. Somehow even his aches and pains seemed to feel good.

Motioning him to follow, the three detectives turned to walk away. Willie hesitated for just a moment before catching up. "Wait a minute," he called out to their backs. "Look out who you're callin' old, hey?"

Game Day

Dan J. Marlowe

1

Tom Jordan awoke on Sunday morning feeling tired. He hadn't been able to fall asleep until late the night before. He got up and walked barefoot in his jockey shorts to the bathroom. He rubbed the purple bruise on his right thigh. It didn't hurt as much this morning. Most of the hard, egg-like lump was gone.

When he came out of the bathroom, his wife, Barbara, was sitting up on the edge of the bed. Her nightgown swelled out because of her near-term pregnancy. "I know you didn't sleep well," she said. "You shouldn't worry so much. You'll do all right in the game this afternoon. You always do."

"That was in college," he said. "This is the pros."

"You'll do all right," she repeated.

"I just wish I was on defense," Tom said. *And that it wasn't my first year,* he thought. "I surely do wish it was defense. I'm not a tight end. I'm a defensive end."

"If you were still on defense, you would have been first in line to be cut," Barbara reminded him. "This way you made the team, and now you're in the starting lineup, even if it did take injuries to get you there."

"There's so much to *remember,*" he said. Tom was silent for a moment, recalling the playbook pages that he had turned endlessly in his mind the night before. *Slot left. Green right. M sideline on two. Drive the linebacker inside. Or slot right. Orange left. Hitch and go on one. Drive the linebacker out.*

Tom shook his head. "When I think that all I had to do before was get to the ball and throw the guy with it across a few yard lines . . . "

"You'll do all right," Barbara said again.

"Yeah, sure," he agreed. "I'm going to get dressed now and ride down to the hotel for the team breakfast."

He showered, finishing off with a cold spray that shocked the 255 pounds on his six-foot, five-inch frame. He dressed quickly in a dark suit, white shirt, and tie. The shirt was tight around his neck and chest. The Marine's exercise program for him was paying off.

"So long," he said to Barbara in the living room. No good-bye kiss on game days was their only superstition.

"Bring me the game ball," she said brightly.

He paused with his hand on the doorknob. "Baby, you've got more brass than a foundry." He smiled. "Here I am, the forty-fifth man on a 45-man squad, and you want the game ball."

"Just bring it to me," she said and smiled back.

Tom didn't say anything. He just stepped out into the hallway and closed the apartment door behind him.

The elevator took him down to the basement garage. He walked over to the old Norton motorcycle he had bought two months ago. He had done so because it was necessary that Barbara have use of the car at all times. He had done a lot of work on the Norton. He fine tuned it until he liked the way it ran.

Their car was getting old, too. It was a four-year-old model he'd bought with alumni help, in his sophomore year in college. That was the summer he and Barbara were married.

Barbara hadn't returned to school after the birth of Susie. Tom himself was still six credit hours short of his degree. He should have done something about it this past summer. Still, it had seemed more important to get himself in shape for the pros.

He glanced at his watch as he rode up the basement ramp to the street. He was early. He had time to ride out to the tri-county training school. He purposely hadn't mentioned it to Barbara. It would upset her, and these days he didn't want Barbara to be upset.

The playbook pages entered his mind again, as he rode along the quiet streets. He was afraid of the pass patterns he had to run from the tight end position. The Marine had made them simple, but he was still afraid. He was more afraid of that than he was of not being able to block the defensive linebacker. He had studied the opposition's Number 55 all week in the game films.

Blocking was a matter of strength. Well, yes, technique, too. Strength he had, but pass catching . . . He ran his tongue over his dry lips. He had never caught a pass in college. He'd never played a down on offense. He'd played defense all the way.

He forced it out of his mind. He turned into the school grounds and rolled along the blacktopped road. There were 2500 patients plus staff inside. He parked the Norton and entered the nursery through the dark-shadowed tunnel from the outpatient department.

2

"Good morning, Mr. Jordan!" a voice said cheerfully, before he even got to the front desk. "Here to see your little girl? Just go right on back to the elevator."

"Thanks," he muttered. During the slow elevator ride upward, his thoughts returned to the line of scrimmage that afternoon and Number 55, the defensive right-side linebacker. Number 55, who moved better to his left than he did to his right. Who was tricky beyond belief. Who fouled when overpowered.

He started down the narrow hallway along the shiny tiled floor. On either side an endless line of cubicles was on display. The cubicles were glassed-in above chest height. This was so the occupants of the six to eight cribs per cubicle could be seen at a glance by passing nurses. Tom avoided looking at the children in the cribs. They were victims of every known birth defect.

He had been told repeatedly that the children could be helped. To a point, at least. He had watched, again and again, as nurses guided babies and small children through exercises designed to make the best possible use of defective limbs.

Barbara hadn't been able to watch without breaking down. After the second visit, he had never brought her again.

He walked faster toward the ward nurse's desk. "Good morning, Mr. Jordan," she greeted him. "Susie's fine and will be glad to see you."

He knew better, but he nodded. The constant atmosphere of cheer almost gagged him at times. Of course, it was necessary for the nurses to set an example for the rest of the help. And for the parents. He turned away from the desk and slipped into the third cubicle on the left. He steeled himself as always against his first look at the tiny child in the middle crib.

Hands clenched, he stared down at his daughter's huge head. The membranes were so delicate they were almost transparent. "Susie is a hydrocephalic," Dr. Carter had explained, when the baby was brought to the training school without ever having left the hospital with Barbara. "In hospital slang, a water head. The condition of her head affects her spine. Her balance is very poor. But we can do things for her here."

"And her—her mentality?" Barbara had asked.

"It will improve."

"Why us, Doc?" he had asked Dr. Carter, when he was first able to accept the white-coated doctor as a person.

"We don't know why, Tom. We're trying to learn. It's been a slow process. But who knows what we might be able to do for these unfortunate children in ten years?"

Ten years . . .

Tom bent down over the crib. He touched the curled little finger of his daughter's hand. There was no response. Susie's brown eyes continued to stare up at the ceiling. Stared as she did hour after hour. *Seeing what,* Tom wondered?

He straightened up quickly and backed away from the crib, blinking his eyes. He went out into the hallway and passed the ward desk. "Thanks," he muttered without breaking stride.

"Thanks for coming, Mr. Jordan," the cheerful voice said.

Ten years . . .

Where would Tom Jordan's marriage be in ten years?

What if the baby Barbara was now carrying turned out to be defective in any way?

It was a subject they never mentioned since Barbara, almost defiantly, had announced her second pregnancy. It hung over them like a cloud every day. He knew that Barbara couldn't stand it. He couldn't stand it. Their marriage couldn't stand it.

3

The Wolves' dressing room shook with the sounds of players putting on their game faces. They were in varying stages of dress and undress. The assistant equipment manager was laying out necessary items in front of each locker. There were ankle bandages, elastic and metal knee supports and braces, and hip and kidney pads.

Partially-dressed players walked nervously through the small spaces. Each one was "getting himself up" for the game in his own way. "Whiskey" Bernardi, the Wolves' best halfback, prowled the room minus his uniform pants. Across the aisle, Roger Newman performed lifting exercises aimed at increasing the 50-inch chest measurement of his 280-pound body. Tom turned around on the bench at a tap on his shoulder. He found himself staring into the blue eyes of the Marine, the offensive line coach. "How you makin' it?" the Marine rumbled.

"Okay," Tom said in a very forced half-whisper. He discarded "perfect" and "great" as meaningless words to use with this smart man.

The Marine nodded. "Come in the trainer's room a minute," he said, and led the way.

The room's only other occupant was Swede Thurlow, the Wolves' quarterback. Fully uniformed, he was sprawled on his back on a training table, his helmet on his chest. Thurlow opened one eye when they entered, then closed it again.

"Number 55 is going to start right out trying to show you who's boss," the Marine said to Tom. "So Swede here will give you a little protection. On our first offensive play, you slide off Number 55 like you can't keep him out. Then run the stop-and-go. Swede will get a pass to you real quick. That'll keep Number 55 on the line of scrimmage for a while, until you can size him up."

Tom swallowed hard. A pass to him on the very first play? The palms of his hands felt damp. "I don't need that," he said.

"You never saw anything like any linebacker in this league in college," the Marine said.

"I can handle him," Tom said.

"But first you'll take the pass," the Marine insisted.

Thurlow opened one eye again. "And when I look for you, rookie, you better be there," he said. He closed the eye again.

"That's all," the Marine said.

Tom walked back to his locker. He tried to blot out the rising tide of noise in the room. He tried to concentrate on the pattern he must run for the stop-and-go. Would Number 55 line up on Tom's right shoulder or his left? When the ball was snapped, would he have to go inside or outside the tough defensive man?

The Marine's sharp bark brought them all to their feet. Tom followed the horde of clattering cleats through the runway. On the field, he had no time to think about anything. The Wolves had won the toss in the pre-game coin flip. On the Lions' kickoff, "Whiskey" Barnardi cradled the spinning football a yard outside the end zone.

Bernardi started upfield with his short, choppy strides. He cut left and right, then was smothered in a cloud of jerseys at the 26-yard line. Tom found himself trotting onto the field next to Roger Newman, the big Number 77, almost before Bernardi hit the ground.

At the Swede's sharp "On two, hike!" Tom wheeled from the huddle to the line of scrimmage. He settled into his stance, glancing to his left at Roger, to make sure he had the right spacing between them. Then he looked across the line for the first time. Number 55 was glaring at him, five yards off Tom's left shoulder.

Despite being keyed up, at the snap of the ball, Tom's charge was a bit slow. He didn't want to be offside. His forward momentum was blunted by Number 55's more explosive charge. The linebacker tried to run right over Tom to get to Swede. Tom bounced off the thrashing body. He crashed into it again to make the man take a longer route to reach Swede. Then, Tom slid off to the inside.

He ran hard for six strides and turned. Swede's arm was already descending and the ball was rocketing right at Tom's chin. He got his hands up and felt the football rebound off his stiff fingers. He watched in horror as it floated loose for an instant. He grabbed at it again, desperately, and pulled it against his chest. He turned upfield, blasting his way past the cornerback trying to angle him to the sideline. He looked for the free safety as he saw a patch of running room, then felt himself cut down at the knees from behind.

He ran back to the huddle, with the sound of his name blaring from the public address system. "Pass caught by Jordan for a 22-yard gain." He thought briefly of Barbara listening to the radio.

The crowd was still buzzing, when Swede brought them out of the huddle again. On left formation, Tom stood in position at the other end of the line, away from Number 55. The play was a trap, and Tom blocked straight ahead on his man, while fullback Buster Moran bolted up the middle for seven yards.

"Watch it!" someone yelled, but it was too late. Fire exploded in Tom's ribs, and he went sprawling. Number 55 had trailed the play and blind sided Tom after the whistle had blown. Roger Newman helped Tom up. "Don't turn your back on that guy," he warned.

Tom struggled back into the huddle. No one looked at him or spoke. Swede called a cutback off-tackle. Tom fired across the line in a rage. Number 55 grabbed him and spun him aside. Then he slowed down Whitey Cuneo enough for the Lion's tackle to slide over and complete the play.

On third-and-five, Swede called for a down-and-out to the split end. Tom dropped off the line to block for Swede. He held off Number 55 at the cost of another elbow in the ribs, but the pass fell short. On the fourth down punt, Number 55 and the safety blitzed Tom, and he barely got a piece of each man. The punter had to hurry his kick.

CHAPTER

4

"He's killing you and you're letting him do it!" the Marine snapped at Tom, on the sideline. Tom crouched down on his heels and tried to hide his rapid breathing. He removed his helmet and wiped his face. He was sweating hard after only the first series.

The Marine squatted beside him, his lean features resembling those of a hawk. "He's putting his hand right in your pocket!" he hammered at Tom. "You got a family to support or don't you, man? You're bigger than he is, so you get out there and show me something!"

Around them, the offensive line surged closer to the sideline. Tom realized that the Lions were in punt formation, after having failed to move the ball against the

Wolves' defense. Tom got up and put his helmet back on. The Marine stood next to him, his face not more than six inches from Tom's. "Get in there and show me you got some guts!" the line coach ordered.

Tom just stared back, and then followed the rest of the team onto the field. He never heard the play that Swede called in the huddle. He flew straight across the line into Number 55. He drove his helmet up into Number 55's chest, and jammed his steel-rod forearms into his belly. The man moved backward six yards, and Tom returned to the huddle with his temperature down a notch.

"Now if you'd just move him in the right direction!" Swede said. Tom didn't care. He knew that the Marine was right. Tom was taller, heavier, and stronger than Number 55. And if he needed to be meaner, he could be that, too. On the next play he hooked Number 55's outside shoulder and hammered him inside. That let Moran cut back through the hole and roll up an 18-yard gain.

Swede moved them steadily downfield with formation right sets, in which Tom slammed into Number 55 with raw power.

Then the veteran quarterback made the line-blasts pay off with a flare pass to Bernardi, who sprinted down the sideline into the end zone. Off the field, the Marine ignored Tom while taking Roger Newman aside for an earnest, low-pitched conversation.

On the next offensive series, Tom settled down to making his mark on Number 55. Tom was handling him consistently now. Again Swede moved them down the field. But on a left sideline pass, in which Tom blocked on the other side of the line, away from Number 55, he relaxed for a moment. The cornerback on that side circled around him and brought Swede down. The Wolves had to settle for a field goal, and Tom returned to the sideline, angry at himself.

The Marine ignored his lapse. "Swede said the nearside cornerback's cheating to help out Number 55 with you," he told Tom. "When he moves in another step, Swede's gonna burn him."

When they went back out on the field, Thurlow called Tom's stop-and-go pattern. Tom slid away from Number 55 and darted into the secondary. The cornerback recovered, though, and was step for step with Tom. Swede calmly fired the ball out of bounds to prevent a possible interception.

Swede called a play to flood the cornerback's zone. Tom ran the same pattern, taking the cornerback with him. Eddie Falconeri, the Wolves' split end, cut across behind them, and picked off Swede's bullet pass. The final 45 yards to the goal line were wide open and he scored untouched.

The first half two-minute warning surprised Tom. He had settled solidly into the rhythm of the game. He was bulldozing Number 55 inside and outside, almost at will. He hadn't been aware of the passing of time. He kept moving around the dressing room during halftime to avoid stiffening up.

"Don't get cocky out there," was the only thing the Marine said to him. Tom knew it was an admission that he was doing all right.

He returned to the field, almost happy. He was only afraid that Number 55 might somehow have gotten his strength back during the intermission. The first set of downs removed that fear. Tom enjoyed himself, as the Wolves racked up another score.

At the start of the final quarter, Number 55 was suddenly gone from the line of scrimmage. Tom went to work on a younger, fresher man. It took him only two sets of downs to show the newcomer who was in charge.

Tom's pleasure in the last ten minutes of the game was spoiled only by the fact that the Wolves failed to score again. When the game was over, the Marine led Tom to a corner of the dressing room. "I wouldn't want you to get the idea you're a tight end, Jordan," he said in his rasping voice. "But you plugged a hole for us. Any man who can do that doesn't need to worry about sending his laundry out for fear he'll be gone before it gets back." And then he walked away.

Most of the players were dressed by the time Tom had showered. "Hey, Jordan!" a voice hailed him. "Want to stop off and have a bite to eat?"

"Maybe another time," Tom replied. "My wife's about to give birth, and I've got to get home."

All during pre-season practice he hadn't mentioned the baby. He didn't want anybody to think he was looking for some sympathy.

But now, being accepted felt sweet.

Everything was looking good.

The new baby would be okay.

Barbara would be okay.

And the doctors would find a way to help Susie.

He reached eagerly into his locker for his clothing.

He couldn't wait to get back to the apartment and tell Barbara about his day.

The Sure Thing

Steve Bradley

1

There was a faraway look in jockey Carmen Solar's eyes, as she stood beside the rail of the racetrack. She was a small and beautiful young woman with large dark eyes and short black hair.

As she watched Fast Dancer run around the racetrack, she dreamed of success.

"He's the fastest thing on four feet," said Carmen's agent, Sam Martin, who stood at the rail beside her.

"I wish I could ride him in the Sullivan Stakes tomorrow," Carmen said, her eyes shining. "I really do."

"Maybe you will get to ride him someday," Sam said.

Carmen's thoughts drifted back in time, as she continued to watch Fast Dancer run.

She thought about her first days at the racetrack as a stable girl. For a long time, she had cleared stables and done all the other dirty work at the track. Then she became a groom. She remembered how she had groomed all the race horses until their coats were bright and felt as soft as silk.

Then she moved up and became an exercise girl. And she had loved all those early mornings alone on the track with just the horse she was riding to keep her company.

Now I am a jockey, she thought. *And someday I'll be the best jockey in the whole country. Maybe in the whole world.*

"One minute and three-fifths seconds," Sam said, as he looked down at the stopwatch in his hand. "That's the best time Fast Dancer has ever made. It's no wonder that he's the favorite in the Sullivan Stakes tomorrow. I'd say he's sure to win."

"I wouldn't," a voice behind them said.

Carmen and Sam turned around to find Dan Blair standing in back of them.

"Good morning, Mr. Blair," Sam said, smiling. "You know Carmen Solar, I believe."

"I do, yes." Blair shook Carmen's hand.

"As a matter of fact, it's Miss Solar I came out to the track to see this morning."

Blair cleared his throat. "Miss Solar, I'd like you to ride my horse, Whirlwind, in the Sullivan Stakes tomorrow."

Carmen was surprised. She looked at Sam, saw his happy smile, and then smiled herself. "I'd very much like to ride Whirlwind for you, Mr. Blair. I'd like to thank you for having faith in me, and giving me the chance to ride a fine horse like Whirlwind."

"I think you're a fine rider," Blair said. "With you in the saddle, I think Whirlwind has a good chance of taking the race away from Fast Dancer. I'll work out the business details of your ride with Mr. Martin. Good luck on Whirlwind tomorrow, Miss Solar."

"Thank you, Mr. Blair." Carmen said good-bye to Sam, and then made her way toward the stables. Suddenly, she started running.

When she came to Whirlwind's stall, she reached out and patted the black horse's neck. "Tomorrow," she whispered. "Tomorrow, it's going to be you and me against the world, Whirlwind. Tomorrow we're going to win the Sullivan Stakes! That's a promise!"

Carmen was still patting Whirlwind's neck, when Sam Martin walked over.

"Oh, Sam!" she cried. "I'm so happy. Why didn't you tell me Mr. Blair was thinking of offering me a mount in the Sullivan tomorrow."

"Because I didn't want to get your hopes up in case it didn't come through. Mr. Blair told me yesterday he was looking for a jockey for Whirlwind and he was thinking of asking you," Sam said.

"Why isn't Mr. Blair's regular jockey riding Whirlwind tomorrow?" Carmen asked.

"Dennis Farrell had an accident at home yesterday. He burned both of his hands. He'll be out of action for several weeks. I heard that Mr. Blair had tried to hire several other jockeys, but all of them already had mounts to ride tomorrow. So he picked you."

"Then I wasn't his first choice to ride Whirlwind."

"No, you weren't. But don't let that fact worry you. He wouldn't have asked you at all if he didn't think you could do a good job. He's pretty sure—and so am I—that you'll finish in the money tomorrow."

"In the money," Carmen repeated. She shook her head. "I don't want to just finish in the money, Sam. Whirlwind and I aren't going to settle for second or third place. We're going to *win* the Sullivan Stakes!"

Later that day, as Carmen was leaving the racetrack, a car pulled up in front of her and a tall man got out.

"Miss Solar," the man said. "I'd like to talk to you for a minute."

"I'm afraid I'm in a hurry, Mr. Carillo," she said, and tried to step around him. Louis Carillo, the heavy gambler, was one person she wanted to stay clear of.

But he blocked her path. "I've heard the good news. The news about you and Whirlwind. Mr. Blair is a smart man. Only a smart man would hire one of the best up-and-coming jockeys on the East Coast."

"If you'll excuse me, Mr. Carillo . . ."

Carillo put out his huge hand and took hold of Carmen's right arm. He pulled her toward him. "I have some news for you, my dear. I have bet a lot of money on the Sullivan Stakes tomorrow—all of it on Fast Dancer to win."

Carmen started to say something, but Carillo wouldn't let her.

"No, don't say anything. Not yet. Let me finish what I have to say to you first."

Carmen nodded and said nothing.

"When I bet on a race, I always bet on a sure thing. Now, in the case of the race tomorrow, I believe that Fast Dancer and his jockey, Billy Crane, *are* a sure thing."

"I don't want to talk about the race, Mr. Carillo."

Carillo's hand tightened on Carmen's arm, almost hurting her. "You don't have to talk about the race—just *listen*— understand."

Carmen tried to break away from Carillo. She couldn't.

"Let me go!" she said.

Carillo didn't let Carmen go. Instead he put his left hand into his pocket. "No other horse in tomorrow's race can come close to beating Fast Dancer—except Whirlwind. He might win with you riding him. But that must not happen."

Carillo's hand came out of his pocket. There was money in it. "I have here one thousand dollars, my dear. It's all yours. Just hold Whirlwind back on the final turn, and keep him from winning. When you have done that, I will pay you two thousand more."

"I don't want your money!" Carmen cried.

"Take it!" Carillo said sharply and put it into the pocket of Carmen's jacket, before she could stop him.

"Look at the matter this way, Miss Solar," Carillo said. "There will be many other races in the days to come. I don't care if you win every one of them. But I don't want you to win the Sullivan Stakes. Is that clear?"

Frightened, Carmen could only nod.

And then Carillo let her go, got in his car, and drove away.

2

That night, sitting in Leo Mendoza's apartment, Carmen was angry—very angry. She looked hard at her boyfriend and said, "I won't throw the race!"

"But you just told me that you were afraid of what Carillo might do, if you crossed him and didn't hold Whirlwind back," he said.

"I don't care!" But Carmen knew she did care. She *was* afraid of what Carillo might do if she crossed him.

"Like Carillo said to you, it's just one race," he said. "No one will ever know that you held Whirlwind back to keep him from winning."

"*I'll* know!" Carmen cried, feeling angry and sad and worried all at the same time.

"Leo . . ." She held his hand. "You know how hard I've worked all these years to become a jockey. Now I am one, and I'm a good one."

"I know you are." Leo leaned over and kissed her. "I know you are a good jockey—one of the best."

Carmen gave him a sad little smile.

"What if someone found out that I'd thrown the race? I would be finished as a jockey."

"No one will ever find out. I'm sure they won't." Leo looked down at his hand in Carmen's. "There is our future together to think about. We need money for that. There is your sister to think about. You said you were going to use part of your next winnings to help her pay her hospital bills. You already have the thousand dollars Carillo gave you and . . ."

"I don't want it, not his kind of money. It's dirty money. I would never have taken it from him, but he put it in my pocket before I could stop him."

"You'll have another two thousand dollars of Carillo's money when the race is over. He said so."

Carmen let go of Leo's hand.

"If you come in second or third in the race, " Leo went on, "you'll have even more money. Carmen, you don't have to win every race. If you place second or third— with your share of the winnings and Carillo's money, you'll have . . ."

Leo fell silent as Carmen got to her feet and crossed the room. She stood with her back to him, looking out the window.

"So you think I should do what Carillo wants, is that it, Leo?"

"I could take the money you and I have saved together and bet it all on Fast Dancer to win. Carmen, we could make a lot of money that way, just like Carillo is going to do. We can, that is, if you hold Whirlwind back. Like Carillo said to you, it would be like betting on a sure thing."

Carmen felt her whole body stiffen. "A sure thing," she said, echoing Leo. Suddenly, she felt cold. She felt something inside her die. She could not turn and look Leo in the eye. Not now, she couldn't. Maybe not ever again.

"Riders up!" The words of the racetrack announcer came over the loudspeaker strong and clear. Carmen swung into the saddle, patted Whirlwind on the neck, and rode out onto the track. The other horses and their riders were all around her.

She fought against the fear she was feeling, as she and Whirlwind made their way to the starting gate. When she reached it, Whirlwind went into the gate without any trouble.

Fast Dancer, with Billy Crane aboard, went in right next to them. "Good luck, Carmen," Billy said.

"Good luck to you too, Billy."

"I don't need any luck," Billy said, confidently. "Not with a great horse like Fast Dancer, I don't."

Seconds later, a loud bell rang.

"They're off!" the announcer shouted through the loudspeaker.

Whirlwind left the starting gate like a bullet fired from a gun. As the horse raced down the track, Carmen bent low over the animal's neck. She held tightly to the whip in her right hand. She kept her booted feet solidly in the stirrups.

The blue and yellow silks of the Blair stables that she was wearing, caught the sun and sparkled. The wind was loud in her ears. Whirlwind's mane, whipped by the wind, flew into her face.

Fast Dancer passed her on the right.

Another horse passed her on the left.

As Carmen rode past the sixteenth post, she caught up to the horse on her left and easily passed him. She didn't hear the cheers from the people in the stands. She only heard the clattering of horses' hooves beneath her.

At the three-quarter-mile post, Carmen looked quickly over her shoulder. One horse was only three lengths behind her. But the others were far back on the track.

Turning her head, she rode on. Now, her eyes were on Fast Dancer, nearly five lengths ahead of her. She knew there was still time to catch up to him.

At that moment, Billy Crane looked back over his shoulder. When he saw Whirlwind, he whipped his horse.

Fast Dancer's speed increased. In a flash, the horse was seven lengths ahead of Whirlwind.

Carmen knew she had to make up her mind—*now*. She thought of all the years she had worked and struggled to become a jockey. And she knew that she couldn't throw all that away. Not for Leo—not for anyone. And certainly not because a man like Louis Carillo had threatened her.

As they came into the final turn, she brought Whirlwind close to the rail. She glanced back once more to make sure she only had one horse to worry about—Fast Dancer. There was nobody behind her for at least eight lengths.

She used her whip on Whirlwind. Once on the right side. Once on the left side.

They gained quickly on Fast Dancer. The lead had been cut to just two lengths. With less than 50 yards to go, the horses were neck and neck.

Then Whirlwind made one final charge and passed Fast Dancer, as the crowd of 45,000 people roared and cheered.

Carmen stood up and waved the whip after she crossed the finish line. She had won the Sullivan Stakes. There was a big smile on her face as she headed for the winner's circle. She was also holding back tears.

She knew she had done the only thing she could do and stay true to herself. But by doing so, she had lost a lot, too.

The money she and Leo had saved—the money he had bet on Fast Dancer—that didn't matter at all to her. But Leo *did* matter to her and she knew that, because of what he had done, she had lost him too.

3

When Carmen left the jockey's dressing room after the race, she was wearing her street clothes. Sam Martin was waiting for her. So was Louis Carillo.

Carmen felt a cold fear at the sight of Carillo, so she moved closer to Sam.

"Your agent," Carillo said to her, "is a smart man."

Carmen wanted to ask Carillo what he meant, but she seemed to have lost her voice.

"Sam Martin is a smart man," Carillo went on, "because he just told me that he bet on Whirlwind to win."

As Carmen looked at Sam, he gave her a big smile.

"And he's not the only smart man around here," Carillo added. "*I* bet on Whirlwind to win, too."

"I'm afraid I don't understand you, Mr. Carillo," Carmen said. "You told me that you were going to bet on Fast Dancer to win. That's why you wanted me to hold Whirlwind back. So that Fast Dancer would be sure to win."

"I told you, my dear," Carillo said, smiling, "that I always bet on a sure thing. I was sure that if I paid you to throw the race, you would do just what you did do. You see, I know what kind of person you are, Miss Solar. I know you are honest. I know you believe in yourself and will do only what you believe is right. I checked you out very carefully before I spoke to you yesterday."

Carmen didn't know what to say. Then she remembered something. She dug into her purse—and came up with the one thousand dollars Carillo had forced on her the day before. She held it out to him.

"Keep it, Miss Solar," he said. "You earned it. You have made me a lot of money because of the way you rode Whirlwind today."

"No, I won't keep it," Carmen said. "I don't approve of you or the way you make your money, Mr. Carillo. I'm happy I won today. But I'm happy for Mr. Blair, who believed in his horse—and in me." Then she put the money in Carillo's hand—this time forcing *him* to take it.

Carillo shrugged his shoulders. "Well, suit yourself," he said. He smiled slightly and walked away.

Carmen turned to Sam. "Thanks for believing in me, Sam. I wish everyone I care for had your faith." She thought of Leo, sadly. She gave Sam a hug and said, "I'll see you tomorrow. Keep getting me those good rides."

As Carmen walked away from Sam, she almost ran into Leo, coming around the corner of the building. He gave her a big smile, and took a stack of bills out of his pocket.

"Is that the money we saved together?" she asked him.

"Yes, it is. But it is much more than that."

Carmen gave him a puzzled look.

"I won almost two thousand dollars on the race," he explained. "I picked the winner."

"You mean that you bet on . . . ?"

"I bet on you and Whirlwind."

"Leo, I . . ."

"I'm sorry I ever thought of asking you to throw the race," he said. "After you left last night, I realized how stupid I was. And I also realized that in the end, there was only one sure thing in the race—*you*."

Carmen almost burst into tears. "I knew I could only ride to win," she said. "But I was afraid that I'd lost you at the same time."

Leo smiled. "You'll always be a winner, Carmen," he said. "And if I'm smart I'll be sure to stay right by your side—forever."

Carmen threw her arms around Leo and hugged him as hard as she could.

Turk

Dan J. Marlowe

1

When the Hawkeyes' shot rebounded from our basket and the ball came directly to Sam, I jumped up from my seat on the bench. The miss had kept the score still tied. Sam whipped a half-court pass to Phil Sheridan, who had half a step on his man. "Go, Phil, go!" I screamed. Nobody ran Phil down from behind on a basketball court.

And then everyone stopped running. The referee was waving off the play. Coach Reardon had called a time-out. I couldn't believe it. With Phil all but free to score the winning basket, Coach Reardon had called time-out. I turned to Ron Elliott standing beside me. "I guess the coach didn't get enough TV time yet," I said.

Elliott heard me. Since the crowd had hushed when they realized what had happened, the whole bench heard me, too, including the coach. His face turned red. Elliott turned away from me, and shook his head.

I looked up at the clock. Nine seconds left. Sure, we could set up a play and have a good chance of making it work. But if the coach hadn't called time, Phil would have had a better chance. I moved out of the way, so the five guys coming over to the bench would have room to kneel down around the coach.

"Williams!" Coach Reardon snapped at me. "Go in for Breed! You inbound the ball!"

I couldn't believe it. I looked down the bench to where Dr. Corell always sat. His seat was empty. Where could Doc be at a moment like this? I hesitated. Doc hadn't given me the OK to test my stress-fractured foot under game conditions yet. I'd only been practicing at about three-quarter speed during the week.

But then it hit me. Here was a chance to play. And play when it counted. I saw

Tommy Breed moving away from the starting lineup. I knelt down in his place. My guard partner when I was playing, Sonny Barcelona, nudged me in the ribs. "Let's do it, Turk," he muttered.

I watched Coach Reardon diagram the play he wanted. Inbounds from me to Sam Jordan, then back to me when I stepped onto the court. I was to look for Bob Fields cutting to the basket and get the ball to him. The second choice was to get it to Sam, our senior forward.

We went out onto the floor. I checked in at the scorer's table and settled myself at mid court, out-of-bounds. The ref was standing four feet away, holding the ball. A jumping jack in a Hawkeye jersey was bounding up and down in front of me, waving his arms, even before the play started.

The ref tossed me the ball. I had timed the jumping jack. When he was on his way down from a jump, I passed the ball to Sonny, who was sprinting toward me. My man turned away, and Sonny got the ball back to me the second I stepped onto the floor. I looked downcourt. Bob Fields was where I expected him to be. He was running slowly, just about inside his opponent's jersey.

Fields would get you 15 to 20 points, any time you didn't need them. When the crunch came, you couldn't find him. He didn't want the ball then. And he made sure he didn't get it. Everyone on the team knew it, except Coach Reardon.

Since I was expecting it, it was no problem. Sam Jordan was cutting toward the basket from the right. I zipped the ball to him. Then I started toward the hoop from the left, running hard, not even thinking about my foot. Sam pulled up, faked a jump shot, shed his man, and popped his shot into the air.

All the bodies were on the other side of the basket. I had a clear lane. Sam's shot looked long. I jumped. I was a foot above the basket when the rebound came off the glass. I hardly had to reach at all. I didn't try to catch it. I slapped it down through the basket with my left hand.

The gym exploded. The guys mobbed me. "Hey, Turk! Hey, Turk!" they were all yelling. The Hawkeyes didn't even think of trying to call a time-out. The game ended. State U. had won a game it wasn't supposed to. One more and we'd be in the play-offs.

Everyone cheered as we ran off the court. I was laughing as we walked down the runway to the dressing room. I couldn't help it. I hadn't even thought I'd get to play. Now the headline would read "STATE SOPHOMORE SINKS WINNING BASKET." I couldn't wait to see Cheryl.

But first I saw Dr. Corell. He came dashing up to me, his face as red as Reardon's had been on the bench. "Who gave you the OK to play?" he shouted. "That foot—who said to try it in a game?"

"Hey, Doc," I protested. "You know who sends the players out onto the floor here."

Silently, he wheeled around and trotted over to Reardon. I could see him bugging Reardon about it, and I could hear Reardon's answer. "Buddy thought he heard you say Williams was ready to play," the coach said easily.

"Buddy" was Buddy Canton, our assistant coach. Doc Corell threw his arms up into the air and walked away. He came back and caught me when I was dressed and ready to leave. "You come to my office in the morning," he ordered. "I want to examine that foot again."

"Sure, Doc," I agreed.

I went out into the runway. Cheryl Hunter was leaning against the opposite wall. She's the Number One player on the women's basketball team. She's not my girlfriend, but I'd like her to be. She's a senior, and a lot of the time she thinks of me as a kid. She never says so, though. And she knows the game and can play it. She's a demon at driving to the hoop. We play a lot of one-on-one in the gym, and I have the bruises to prove it.

"Well, hero," she greeted me. "How in the world did you ever get into the game? The way coach Reardon feels about your fast-running mouth even when you're healthy, I never expected to see it."

"Neither did I," I admitted. "Maybe he was giving me a chance to fall on my face, putting me in cold?"

"I wouldn't go that far," Cheryl said.

"Although he had a tie game. The worst he was going to get was overtime. I wonder."

Cheryl didn't like Reardon any better than I did. I took her arm and we started out for post-game hamburgers. "He hasn't liked you since the first week of practice, in your freshman year," she continued.

That was when I'd made my mark on Coach Reardon. He liked to practice with the players the first couple of weeks, before they really got into shape. We'd been playing three-on-three, with him guarding me. I'd had to inbound a pass, almost like in tonight's game. Reardon was crowding me even more than the guy tonight.

"Pass the ball! Pass the ball!" he kept yelling, right in my face. I tried to move him back and he wouldn't move. So I slammed the ball right off his foot. It came back to me and I picked it up and made the inbound pass. It left Reardon on the floor holding his foot, trying not to show he was in pain. Reardon was wrong, and I was wrong, but there it was. I had nobody crowding me on inbound passes after that.

It had cost me, though. I'd come to State U. as a forward. A week later Reardon told me I was a guard. He had decided that Bob Fields was going to play the forward spot I had already marked off as mine. I must have spent a thousand hours in the gym learning to play guard.

It's funny how things work out. I'd been a medium-sized forward at six feet five inches. That height made me a big guard. By sophomore year, I'd become the point guard, running the team. And I could always shoot. Reardon had done me a favor without either of us realizing it. But then halfway through the season, I'd gotten hurt, and it was nothing but bench time after that.

I told Cheryl that I would be seeing Doc Corell in the morning. "I hope he lets me play on Saturday," I said.

What makes you think Reardon would play you even if Doc okayed it, Turk? I don't think Reardon feels it's necessary to make you a star."

"Don't be so cheerful," I told her.

2

The next morning, I met Doc Corell at his office. He examined the foot and took X-rays again. He kept grunting to himself while he studied the slides against a strong light. "Much better," he said finally. "It's healed very well."

"Does that mean I can play Saturday, Doc?"

He hesitated. "All right," he said finally. "But only for short periods of time."

"Great!" I said. "Thanks, Doc."

Coach Reardon's office was just down the hallway from the doctor's. I knocked once on his door and opened it. Reardon was sitting at his desk with Sandy Martin, the sports editor from the local newspaper.

"Excuse me," I apologized. "Coach, I just wanted to let you know that Doc says I can play on Saturday."

"You're not in shape, Williams," Reardon replied.

"You mean you won't play him after what he did for you last night?" Martin spoke up. He was grinning at me.

"Oh, if the flow of the game calls for it, I will . . . ," Reardon said, his voice trailing off. He was always worried about newspaper criticism. Any kind of criticism. Which was why I had never been very high on his list of favorites.

I waved to Martin and went down the hall. Passing the gym, I heard the thump-thump-thump of a basketball. I knew who it was, even before I opened the door. Sonny Barcelona was dribbling and shooting baskets between classes.

"Hey, man!" he greeted me. "You really showed Reardon up last night. The guys thought it was great."

"You think I was supposed to blow it?"

"He sure didn't think you were going to win it." Sonny had been smiling, but then he turned serious. "Say, did you hear that Fields is showing a junior college hotshot around campus? He's putting him up over the weekend."

"Why? Reardon doesn't have any scholarships to give next year, even to the best junior college player in the country. He's used up his quota."

"Suppose he took back one of his current scholarships?"

"Hey, Sonny, you're not exactly making my day. Have you heard anything?"

"No, but why else is the guy here? Reardon would love to bring in someone to make Fields look good. Make Reardon look good, too."

"Instead of showing him up like I do? Yeah, I see what you mean. Me and my big mouth. He's such a big fat target, though. I just can't help letting air out of his balloon."

"Want to shoot around?" Sonny asked, offering me the ball.

"No, thanks. See you later."

I had an hour until my Spanish class started.

I crossed the campus to Cheryl's dormitory. I needed some advice. She had a head on her shoulders. All I seemed to have was a mouth.

*   *   *

Cheryl was in the lounge, reading. She put down her textbook when I came in. "Trouble?" she asked right away. She doesn't have much difficulty reading the looks on my face.

I explained to her about the hotshot on campus as a possible transfer, plus Reardon just about telling me I wasn't going to play Saturday night. "Do you think I'm paranoid to feel Reardon could be loading up the toe of his boot for me, Cheryl?"

"No," she said thoughtfully. "No, I don't. In view of the manner in which you go out of your way to annoy him."

"He invites it, Cheryl. Personality aside, he's not even a good coach."

"But you need him if you're serious abut getting your degree."

"You bet I'm serious. I'll never make it in the pros. I'd like to be a starter here, but I don't have any crazy dreams about a pro career."

"Then you've got to convince Reardon he needs you. Or that he'd run into too much trouble trying to get rid of you. Knowing him, that would probably work better. What's involved in pulling a scholarship?"

"Well, it's seldom done outright. If he's planning it, Reardon probably feels he could get away with it by saying my injury makes me too much of a risk for next year. But it's not like they say, 'You're fired.' Instead they set up four or five hundred circumstances, all nasty, to make you quit. Pile things up on you until you quit."

"Couldn't you sit tight and outlast him?"

"I've seen guys try it. It doesn't work. They turn things around so that even your own teammates feel you're hurting the team by not moving on. They can really put pressure on you."

"And with your famous temper. . . ." Cheryl was tapping a pencil against her teeth. "We've got to think this through. You know, Turk, you've got yourself to blame for a lot of this."

"A nice guy like me?"

She ticked off her fingers one after another. "As an athlete, you're arrogant and you have a bit of a mean streak. Which isn't all bad. But as a human being Turk . . ."

"Being modest doesn't become me, Cheryl."

"It's going to have to become you if you're planning to stay in school. Or you're going to need enough leverage . . . ," she paused, with her pencil tapping again. "Let me think about it," she said.

I went on to my Spanish class.

When I got back to my room in the athletic dorm, there was note for me to stop in at assistant coach Buddy Canton's office. I looked at it with a chill feeling in my stomach. Could they really do this to me?

I telephoned Cheryl.

CHAPTER

3

I sat across from Buddy Canton's desk, watching him give me the evil eye. He wasted no time. "We don't think you can cut it any more, Williams," he laid it on the line.

"You're wrong," I told him. *Don't say too much,* Cheryl had warned me. *Just enough to make your points.*

"Plus your attitude is bad," Canton continued. I didn't say anything. "And that spoils the team's attitude."

"I don't happen to think so."

"We think you're . . ."

"What about my scholarship?" I cut him off.

Canton shrugged. "You wouldn't want to stick the school for a free ride, would you?"

"Are you saying I'm physically unable to play?"

Cheryl had said they were too smart to make any flat statements. "We're saying that for the good of the team . . . ," Canton began.

"I'm staying, Canton," I said, cutting him off again. "For all four years." I could see Canton was puzzled. Based on past performance, he had probably expected me to go over the desk after him. And if it hadn't been for Cheryl, I probably would have. That would have given them all the reason they needed to dump me.

He turned as red as a soft tomato.

"We're saying that you won't enjoy it," he said, stiffly.

"Are you speaking of harassment? Lack of playing time?"

"We're saying you won't enjoy it," he repeated.

I got tired of it. I reached across his desk and pulled his phone toward myself. Then I dialed Sandy Martin's number at the newspaper, which I had printed on my palm just before entering Canton's office. "Hi, Sandy," I said to the sportswriter, when he came on the line. "This is Turk Williams."

"Hi, Turk," he responded. "What's up?"

"I'm holding a press conference Saturday night after the game, Sandy," I said. "I hope you'll be there. It has to do with the basketball program here at State U. I think you'll find it interesting," I finished, with a smile at Canton.

"What's the main thrust going to be?"

"No hints. Except you could call it a view from inside."

"Wouldn't miss it," he said. "I'll spread the word around."

"Thanks," I said, and hung up the phone. I shoved it back across the desk. "Tell Coach Reardon he's invited. You, too."

Buddy Canton was about to explode. "Do you think a jerk kid like you can blackmail us?" he demanded angrily.

"Not if you don't mind the truth coming out about the way you and Reardon run the program," I said.

"You'll never play basketball here or anywhere else!" he threatened.

Despite Cheryl's warning, I lost my temper. "If I don't play, you won't coach," I promised him. "I'm not going to roll over and play dead for you."

I got up and walked toward the door.

"Don't forget to shave Saturday night," I needled him, on my way out. "There'll probably be some guys there covering it for TV."

I started Saturday night's game. Reardon had caved in, just as I'd known he would. I couldn't breathe after five minutes, and had to take myself out of the game. Reardon looked happy. But I gave him the eye when my throat and chest loosened up, and he put me back in. After that it was all right.

The guys were doing everything they could to make me look good. Sam Jordan and Phil Sheridan were cutting for the basket all night. I'd drive to the hoop, then dish it off, and they'd go up and score. They scored so often that they ran up my assist total. With three baskets by Sonny, from long range after passes from me, my assists at the half numbered thirteen. It wasn't an unlucky number.

Cheryl had brought along half of the girls from her sorority house. Every time I touched the ball, they cheered. They got the crowd into it, too. After a while, all I had to do was scratch my nose and I was cheered.

What could have been a tough game turned into a laugher. The easy win put us into the conference tournament. That meant I'd get to play at least three more games even if we didn't win it. Enough to prove to everyone that I could play. I even made half a dozen baskets myself, as if to emphasize the point.

We hadn't discussed it, but it was understood that if I played, I wouldn't blow the whistle about the program. Still, Reardon looked nervous when we reached the dressing room and saw the reporters and the cameras.

"Clothes on, guys," I told the team. "We're going to have women among us."

Cheryl led some of her gang into the room. The photographers were surprised. Then, they figured they had better start snapping pictures of the young women. This was Cheryl's idea, too. "If you play, and you can't blast Reardon and Canton, you'll still need something for the press conference," she had pointed out.

I introduced her to the press, and she took over. Her sorority, Kapp Pi Alpha, was setting up a program to tutor student-athletes who needed it, she announced. It would be an ongoing and open-ended program. And it would result in a greater number of athletes getting enough credits to graduate.

There was a polite pause.

It wasn't what the assembled press had expected.

"And it's at Coach Reardon's suggestion that this program is being started," Cheryl added.

Reardon looked startled, but then beamed and aimed his best profile at the cameras.

I could never have brought myself to say that last part, but Cheryl's a politician. "You go along to get along," she'd told me. "It's time you grew up."

So I guess I'm growing up.

I couldn't truthfully say I'd become humble. But after what I'd just been through, I'll guarantee I was less arrogant than before.

You never appreciate what you have until you're faced with losing it.